Crown of Thorns

A Scarlett Bell Thriller

Dan Padavona

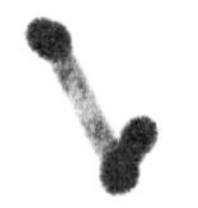

Copyright Information

Published by Dan Padavona

Visit our website at www.danpadavona.com

Cover Design by eBookLaunch

Crown of Thorns

CHAPTER ONE

Scarecrows don't move. Of that, Shelly LaFleur was certain.

LaFleur shaded her eyes and stared over the corn, a field of verdant green that stretched a football field's length into the westering sun. Leaves flapped like skittish birds. Insurgent weeds sprouted among the paths and hunched over where she'd shoved them aside during the morning rounds.

The scarecrow hung above the center of the field. Two black crows perched on either arm and squawked, not phased by LaFleur's faux watchman. So it hadn't been the scarecrow she saw moving through the field. So what was it? A shadow, perhaps. Or maybe she was overdue for new prescription glasses. Whatever it had been, it was gone now. She shrugged away momentary uneasiness and set off for the barn.

A wind borne of the Gulf, gummy and suffocating, slithered through the field and stuck to her face. It was too hot, too sultry for early June in Northern New York. If this was a sign of things to come, she wouldn't be able to breathe come August.

Though slashes of shadows cloaked the inside of the barn, the heat felt worse inside, the hay and baked wood scents overwhelming. No wind, the air pent up and stagnant, a dead thing.

She snatched up an old bucket of hay and alfalfa and walked it over to the horse stall, where Winnie paced and pawed at the door latch.

"Hungry, girl?"

LaFleur offered a handful to the horse. The old mare dipped its face into her hand, the horse's teeth and tongue tickling her palm as it fed.

The mare neighed as she set the bucket down.

"Easy now. I'll let you into the pasture as soon as I'm sure a storm ain't brewin'. "

To LaFleur, it seemed a storm hid on the horizon, somewhere over Lake Ontario. She sensed it the way one does eyes on her back, a distant energy that wanted to unleash its fury on the lake plain. But as she stepped out of the barn and surveyed the hills, she saw only hazy blue and the shredded contrail from a long departed airliner.

The sensation of being watched grew when she returned to the corn. Though the rows needed clearing before the field became an impassable jungle, she found it difficult to put one foot in front of the other. An unidentifiable fear.

Shadows in the corn. An unseen storm over the lake.

These were the paranoid worries of a woman who spent too much time by herself. No husband, no child. The concept of a nuclear family never appealed to her. The farm was all the family she needed, just the earth and the seasons to keep her company.

She liked it this way, though the men outside the general store whispered about her, and the locals held pity in their eyes when they visited her booth at the farmers market as though she were a charity case. No matter as long as they kept buying.

She was halfway up the tractor when the scarecrow leaped off the cross and plunged into the corn. LaFleur caught her breath, uncertain what she'd seen. The crows winged off in opposite directions while the perch wobbled with unspent momentum.

The scarecrow had fallen before, but she was sure she'd secured it well. Damn crows probably pecked at the ropes. The irony might have provoked laughter were she not a bundle of nerves.

Not chancing the possibility of some animal prowling through the field, she grabbed her rifle off the back of the tractor. After retrieving rope from the barn wall, Winnie fretful and strutting around her stall, LaFleur started toward the field, looking at the empty perch with annoyance and a terror she couldn't place.

Inside the rows, the growing stalks emitted rich scents which always brought her back to childhood days spent on her parents' farm. An only child, she'd busied herself with chores, the fantasy adventures she concocted in her head a substitute for friends. Sometimes she explored rainforest jungles or explored the darkest reaches of Mordor. Mom and Dad found her a tad odd, but no one worried over her imagination provided she finished her work and kept her grades up in school.

Solitude was a gift, not a disease or a reason for the townsfolk to take pity on her.

Fighting through the overgrown weeds, LaFleur

made it to the middle of the field. The scarecrow lay face down, arms splayed as if it had belly-flopped off a diving board to nowhere. The crows circled and cawed in the sky.

Unraveled rope lay to either side of the scarecrow. Frays in the fibers suggested someone cut the scarecrow down. But why? She gripped the rifle, sweat trickling into her eyes. Kids might play a practical joke, but the scarecrow stood too tall for a child to reach.

The stalks shifted behind her. She spun and pointed the rifle into the corn.

"Who's in there?"

Even with the sun strong on the horizon, darkness curled among the rows.

"Come out now. That was a fine trick you played, but the joke's over."

Her voice wavered, belying the courage of her words. And the noise came again. A parting of the stalks as though someone circled her.

"That's enough. Show yourselves, or I'm calling the sheriff."

LaFleur hauled the scarecrow into her arms. It slumped over her shoulder, lifeless, black eyes glaring into the rows. She spat and hoisted the scarecrow onto its perch and tied the rope around one of its arms. Then she started to secure the next, one eye sweeping through the sea of green as the stalks danced and swayed with the growing wind.

Irritated over the scarecrow, she forgot her fears and let down her guard. The rifle stood on end, propped up against the post, when the thing crashed out of the corn. At first, she saw a goat's head and thought someone's pen had busted, but the head stood too tall above the rows.

LaFleur grasped for the rifle as the monster tore out of the corn. The sight of the goat-headed man stunned her. She pulled the trigger as he pummeled her head with a knife hilt. The rifle thundered and kicked back against her shoulder.

The hilt battered her skull while she kicked and thrashed beneath the man's weight. He leered down at her. Eyes wild, crazed.

Behind him, the scarecrow dangled by one arm. The last thing LaFleur saw was the dead goat eyes glaring down at her. Then the hilt smashed her between the eyes, and the sky went black.

When LaFleur ceased moving, the man removed the goat's head and placed it beside her. He removed a video camera from his shoulder and focused the lens on the farmer's sleeping face.

And he began to film.

CHAPTER TWO

Special Agent Scarlett Bell grabbed the door handle when Neil Gardy took the curve too fast. His brown hair speckled by gray, Gardy eased off the gas and avoided turning the rental into a ditch.

"Trying to lap the field, Dale Earnhardt?"

Gardy eased off the gas and clicked off the satellite radio.

"I forgot how much these back roads twisted. Hey, aren't you the one with the lead foot?"

"For the record, I've never put us in a ditch. Or hit a tree for that matter."

Gardy snickered his Muttley the cartoon dog laugh.

"That tree was completely out of place."

"In a forest, yes."

An hour ago, they'd landed at Syracuse airport with a strong sense of deja vu. A year earlier, the two FBI Behavioral Analysis Unit agents captured serial killer Alan Hodge at nearby Coral Lake. Now they raced against the setting sun to reach the rural village of Golden, situated a stone's throw from the glistening blue waters of Lake

Ontario.

Gardy tapped the case file on Bell's lap.

"Our contact is Sheriff Kemp Marcel."

She screwed up her face as if she'd bit down on a lemon.

"Why do I sense another border war with local law enforcement brewing?"

"Stay positive. Coral Lake is the next county southward. Different sheriff."

"He find the victim?"

"She didn't show for the farmer's market last Saturday and stopped answering her phone. Sheriff went out to have a look and found...well, you'll just have to see how he found her. It's not pretty."

Bell paged through the case notes.

"Shelly LaFleur, farmer on the outskirts of Golden, New York."

"Sheriff says she's a bit of a recluse. Except for market, nobody saw her. Thing is, the farmer's market was her livelihood. She never missed a day."

"Until last Saturday."

Green hills accented by wildflowers rolled past in colorful streaks. With the windows open, the scents traveled into the rental SUV and brought to mind childhood days in Bealton, Virginia when school let out for the summer. The undulating terrain looked similar to Coral Lake, but without the population. This was God's country, a place industry wouldn't discover for another few centuries, if ever.

Gardy turned down a dirt and gravel road, the stones loud beneath the SUV. Tree-covered hills grew as far as the eye could see. Atop one ridge, a trio of windmills twirled over the countryside like benevolent giants. She could hear them with the windows rolled down, the sound pleasing compared to the static from the AM radio.

The occasional farm sprang out of the wilderness. A road sign proclaimed Golden lay only two miles ahead as they came upon a tractor heading in the opposite direction. The face of the tractor driver was shriveled and parched from decades in the sun. He eyed the agents and gave an almost imperceptible tilt of his hat as the two vehicles passed.

"This is it," said Gardy, stomping on the brakes when an unmarked road popped up on their left.

In a swirl of dust, the rental plodded down another dirt road. Bell couldn't see more than ten yards in front of the vehicle until the dust settled. A cornfield and old barn appeared down the road as though a London fog parted. Something hung suspended above the crop. A scarecrow, Bell thought, but too bulky to be a dummy. Crows set down upon the arms and pecked.

The victim. Bell's stomach flipped.

She leaned forward for a better view and pointed at a truck parked between the barn and field.

"There's the sheriff's vehicle."

Gardy, also staring at the macabre scarecrow, rubbed at his eyes and turned into the driveway. Two more sheriff department trucks stood beside a white farmhouse, and the county coroner's wagon, ebony and hearse-like, sat parallel to the field. The elderly female standing with her arms folded looked out of place beside the sheriff and his three male deputies. Bell wondered if the woman was the county medical examiner. They all turned their eyes toward the agents.

After Gardy killed the engine, the only sounds were the dying breeze and the murmured voices of the deputies. They fell silent when Gardy and Bell stepped out of the SUV.

Bell's eyes traveled between the officers and LaFleur's house. The home was recently painted, quaint and homey on the outside. A long porch welcomed visitors, though Bell figured she could count on one hand the number of people who called on LaFleur. One lonely rocking chair seemed to move on its own when the wind set the corn in motion.

The oldest of the officers, an imposing figure with a wavy spill of gray below his hat, stepped forward.

"Agents Gardy and Bell, I presume. I'm Sheriff Marcel. Thank you for coming so quickly."

Gardy shook his hand.

"Neil Gardy."

Marcel nodded and offered his hand to Bell. His skin felt calloused, grip firm.

"Scarlett Bell."

The twinkle in Marcel's eye told Bell he knew of her.

"A pleasure. These are my deputies: Monteville, Rasovich, and Greene. And our county medical examiner, Dr Nadia Collings."

The three deputies stood back and eyed the agents. Collings approached Bell and greeted her as if anxious to free herself of the old boy network.

"Not to cut the formalities short," said Gardy, peering over the stalks to where the sun plunged toward the horizon. "But we'd better get moving before we lose daylight."

Kemp removed his hat and fidgeted, wiping his

forehead with his sleeve.

"Maybe it would be better if you came with us, Agent Gardy, and Agent Bell accompanied Deputy Greene to the farmhouse."

Bell fought the urge to chew her lip. Gardy shook his head.

"If anyone should view the body, it's Agent Bell. Nobody profiles serial killers better."

Marcel raised his hands.

"I'm certain what you say is true, but once you see the body—"

Bell threw her evidence bag over her shoulder.

"Thanks for the concern, Sheriff, but like Agent Gardy said, we're losing the sun."

Marcel paused, searching for a reason to exclude Bell. Then he shrugged and stepped onto the pathway.

"Follow me."

Weeds choked the path and tripped them up. Beneath the stalks, animals skittered away at their approach. Monteville and Rasovich yammered about last night's baseball scores and whether the Yankees had enough pitching to win the series this year. Greene, the youngest of the deputies, followed at their heels, a puppy dog seeking approval.

It took several minutes to fight their way through the rows, the post holding the scarecrow tauntingly poking up from the field. The anticipation magnified the tension, forced Bell to steel herself from the inevitable horror. If she quaked before Marcel, she'd vindicate his belief that she should have remained back at the farmhouse. A woman's place is in the kitchen, she pictured him saying.

Collings gasped before Bell realized they'd broken

into the clearing. The pale, naked body of Shelly LaFleur hung in place of the scarecrow. Distended. Face purple, tongue lolling outward like a curious worm. Finally at a loss for words, Monteville and Rasovich studied their shoelaces. Greene placed his hands on his hips and turned back to the stalks as if searching for a lost piece of evidence. For Marcel's part, he removed his hat and performed the sign of the cross.

Bell caught her breath. Something wrapped around LaFleur's forehead. Dried blood streaked the woman's face down her nose and cheeks.

"What the hell is on her head?"

She edged closer.

"It's a crown of thorns," Marcel said, cupping his hand over his mouth.

Gardy met the sheriff's gaze.

"You a religious man, Sheriff?"

The sheriff made a gruff sound in his chest and wandered to the corpse. Bell followed, and Marcel looked despairingly at her.

"I warned you," said Marcel as Bell clicked photographs.

After Bell finished, she removed her phone and dictated notes. Later she'd transcribe the audio to paper and begin the profile of the murderer.

"The unknown subject tied the victim's forearms to the crossbar. The bar must be...six or more feet off the ground. Wouldn't you say, Sheriff?"

The sheriff broke out of his daze.

"Sounds about right." Marcel stood beside the crossbar, careful not to touch the corpse. "Yes, I'd say six feet."

Marcel stammered through his reply, his face peaked. Bell kept the sheriff talking and nudged him back into the investigation.

"So our killer must have been a good sized man."

Marcel nodded and swiped the sweat off his brow.

Gardy craned his head up at LaFleur. Thorns cut into the woman's flesh, her skin punctured and torn.

"What do you think, Bell? Do we have another visionary killer on our hands?"

Marcel scrunched his face.

"Visionary killer?"

"It's possible. Visionary killers," Bell explained for Marcel, "often experience breaks with reality. Some claim to take orders from God or Satan."

"Like the God's Hand killer?"

Bell muttered an affirmative, wishing Marcel hadn't brought up the serial killer who murdered her childhood friend.

"Yes, you could say that."

"Heaven help us if a serial killer like that is running loose in Golden."

The original scarecrow lay beneath the stalks, legs extended into the clearing. The three deputies converged on the scarecrow to search for evidence. Likely to put distance between them and the corpse.

"Don't touch the scarecrow," she said as she circled behind LaFleur.

Rasovich, the oldest of the officers turned his pockmarked face toward Bell.

"How's that?"

"Not without gloves. If you don't have your own, Agent Gardy can provide you with a pair."

Rasovich grumbled under his breath, poking at the scarecrow with his shoe as if it might come to life.

"You gonna cut her down?" Marcel asked, swinging his hat at a pair of crows. "Don't seem right."

Bell clicked another set of pictures before she allowed the deputies to untie the ropes. They all wore gloves now, Rasovich's face twisted in revulsion as he and Monteville lowered the woman.

"How long will it take you to determine cause of death?" Marcel asked Collings.

The doctor knelt beside LaFleur's corpse and studied bruises around the mouth and nose.

"The sooner I get her onto my table, the better," Collings said, waving away a swarm of gnats.

Bell ran her eyes over the field. So many places to hide. She wondered how long the killer watched LaFleur before he struck. No obvious trails existed through the corn, and the loss of daylight didn't help matters.

The first stars flickered as night swooped down on the farm. They were almost back to the farmhouse when Gardy's phone rang.

"Yeah, Harold."

Bell glanced at her partner as he spoke. A phone call from Harold was unusual. Gardy or Bell phoned the BAU technician when they required deep background checks traditional law enforcement databases couldn't provide.

Gardy stopped and held up his hand. The deputies shared worried glances.

"Okay, send it to me now."

Gardy needn't have asked the others to gather around. They'd already formed a circle around the agent. He clicked on the link Harold sent him. While they peered over his shoulder, a photograph of LaFleur appeared on the screen as they'd discovered her. The lighting looked different, harsh and bright with the afternoon sun, but the similarity was enough for Gardy to wheel around and stare into the field.

"Can't you trace the picture?" Marcel asked. "Find who uploaded it, and we'll have our killer."

Harold's voice came over the speaker.

"No go, Gardy. Whoever set this up is good. Damn good. He's bouncing the hosting site through multiple servers. I haven't been able to locate the source."

"Keep working at it, Harold. Call me as soon as you know something."

Bell studied the picture, then shook her head.

"Brazen. He wants the world to see what he did."

"How'd your people find the website in the first place?" Marcel asked, averting his eyes from the picture.

Gardy glanced pensively at the screen.

"He emailed the FBI."

CHAPTER THREE

The County Coroner's Office was situated in a long, gray brick building with blue shingles. The office lay twenty-seven miles south of Golden, and the drive took nearly an hour in the dark along rural roads.

Bell's phone rang as they pulled into a parking space near the entryway.

"It's my mother," Bell said.

Gardy cut off the engine.

"You better take it."

"You sure?"

"It's your mother. Of course, you should take it. I'll be inside."

"Thanks a million. I'll be right behind you. This won't take more than a minute."

Bell eyed the phone skeptically. Usually when Tammy Bell called, she made it a point to critique her daughter's career choice. Sighing, Bell answered.

"Everything okay, Mom?"

"Yes, everyone's fine. You aren't on another case, are you?"

"As a matter of fact, I am," Bell said, climbing out of the SUV. She leaned against the door and let the night air —fresh and cool unlike Virginia in June—tickle her awake. "We flew into New York this afternoon."

Tammy Bell harrumphed.

"It seems the FBI should give you a little vacation time, especially after you caught Jillian's killer and saved the congresswoman's daughter. It's like they don't care about your wellbeing. If you don't stand up for yourself, Scarlett, they'll take advantage of you."

"Was there a reason you called, Mom?" Bell asked, shifting the phone to her other ear.

"Oh, right. Listen, honey, I don't want you to take this the wrong way, but your dad and I have been talking, and it's time we had a change a scenery."

"A change in scenery? What are you talking about?"

Tammy Bell cleared her throat.

"Bealton isn't what it used to be, and we found a beautiful little retirement community outside of Phoenix."

Bell paced the parking lot, the lamplight harsh in her confused state.

"Phoenix. As in Arizona?"

"Well, yes."

"All of this seems rather sudden. What will you do with the house?"

"Sell it, of course. I realize this is a bit of a shock to you, but Dad and I talked about this for years. He's retired. All of our friends have moved on. There's nothing keeping us in Virginia."

Nothing keeping you here except your daughter, Bell said to herself. She regretted the thought. It was selfish, and her parents didn't require her blessing. Bell blew the hair out of her eyes.

"What about Dad's adenoma?"

"Your father is healthy, dear. And they have doctors in Arizona."

"But he'll be starting over with a doctor who doesn't know his health history. Shouldn't he stick with his current doctor until they're sure the coast is clear?"

"Scarlett, we're approaching sixty. I'm sure you don't want to hear this, but the coast will never be clear in the coming years. Which is exactly why we want to do this. While we still can."

Her back against the lamppost, Bell kicked at a pebble. It made a hollow, lonely sound as it bounced across the parking lot.

"I wish you'd think about this a little longer."

"We didn't make this decision overnight, Scarlett."

Gardy paced inside the entryway. Bell tapped her foot.

"I've gotta go, Mom. Let's talk about this when I get back."

She hated ending the call like this. Her mother's timing couldn't have been worse, and once Tammy Bell made up her mind, there was no changing it. Bell clicked the key fob and locked the rental.

The inside of the County Corner's office was well-lit and vacant. Potted plants did little to break up the monotony of the white, antiseptic hallways. The examining room waited at the end of the corridor. Gardy checked his phone outside the door when Bell approached. He glanced up when she drew near.

"Everything okay?"

Bell shook her head.

"Yes. No. I'm not sure."

"That covers the bases."

Bell stuffed her hands into her pockets.

"Lead the way, Kemosabe."

Dr Collings slipped on a pair of gloves as Bell followed Gardy into the examining room. The medical examiner regarded them over her glasses. The body of Shelly Lafleur lay face down upon a stainless steel table which reflected the spotlight like a noonday sun.

Bell put on a pair of gloves, too, and walked to the table opposite Collings.

"What have you determined, doctor?"

"I estimate the time of death at twenty-four hours ago. Suffocation. Notice the bruise marks around the mouth." Collings lifted LaFleur's chin and opened an eyelid. "The eyes are bloodshot, another indication the killer suffocated the victim. Furthermore, I found carpet fibers under her nails."

Collings reached up and redirected the light as Bell leaned closer. The fibers could have come from LaFleur's own carpet, but Bell doubted it. To be certain, they'd test the fibers against those found inside the farmhouse.

"Anything else?"

"Yes. Look at the victim's back."

Bruising stretched across the width of the victim's back.

"Lividity suggests her back lay against a rough surface when the killer suffocated her," Bell said.

Collings nodded.

"I pulled two splinters off her back."

"What about the pole?" Gardy asked. Bell knew he agreed with her assessment but felt a need to test her.

"Couldn't her body banging against the pole when the wind blew cause the lividity?"

"No, the markings suggest a wider surface. Something wooden. The pole was no bigger than my fist, and if you look closely, you can see the faint outline from where the body met the metal. On the other hand, lividity is at least twice as large." Bell bent low and examined the skin for additional trace evidence. "But you bring up an important point. The fact that the pole outline is so faint tells me she was dead for nearly twenty-four hours before he hung her."

"He keeps the bodies before he displays them to the world."

The doctor's attention swung between their volleys. She cocked an eyebrow.

"Bodies. Are you saying he's done this before?"

"Or he will again," said Bell, studying LaFleur's neck for indications the killer choked her. There were none.

"So he's a serial killer."

"Yes, though he recently began killing."

"First that crazy man in Coral Lake last year, now this. It doesn't seem possible."

"Doctor," said Gardy, snapping a photo of the lividity markings. "Have you witnessed any suspicious deaths over the last year near Golden?"

"No, nothing like this."

"It wouldn't necessarily be this extreme. It's possible the killer's violence escalated after he gained a taste for killing."

"No suffocations, no suspicious deaths. And I certainly would have remembered a crown of thorns." Dr Collings twisted her mouth. "There is one thing. This wouldn't come across my desk, but my sister-in-law lives in Golden, and she mentioned several dogs went missing during the last year. For a while, the sheriff's department figured someone stole them for dogfighting." Collings noted the meaningful glance Bell gave Gardy. "What? Do you think the crimes are related?"

"It's worth looking into," said Bell. "Sometimes serial killers start with animals, pets, then work their way to humans."

Collings, a woman who didn't appear easily rattled, shuddered.

"Talk to Sheriff Marcel. He'd know about the missing dogs."

CHAPTER FOUR

Eyes burning from lack of sleep, feet dragging, Bell dropped her bag on the motel room bed and fell into a chair. So much for five-star accommodations. The Golden Lion Motel stashed itself on a country route outside of Golden. Eight rooms and a vending machine. A blinking vacancy sign with two letters out. Nothing but darkness in all directions. Bell hadn't heard a car engine since they arrived.

They'd awakened the manager from a deep sleep upon arrival, his feet on the desk, some grainy slasher movie streaming on the computer screen. The FBI badges jostled the manager. He twice dropped the keys—no modern cards at this motel—and botched the forms. Bell wondered if he had anything to hide or if two feds bursting into his office an hour before midnight provided ample intimidation.

For once, she'd won the argument. Gardy grudgingly allowed Bell to have her own room despite the threat of serial killer Logan Wolf stalking her across the country.

Gardy's room neighbored hers, and a locked

adjoining door provided access between the two rooms. Bell didn't plan to open that door unless Godzilla came stomping through the L-shaped motel. She brushed the hair out of her eyes, slid off her pants and shoes, and pulled on a pair of gray sweatpants and sneakers, heaven after the pant suit and heels. A moment after she pointed the remote at the television, her phone buzzed. Gardy had returned with dinner, if you could call fast food burgers and fries dinner. She was hungry enough to eat anything, and out in the middle of nowhere, beggars couldn't be choosers.

Gardy spread the food out on a corner table. Bell entered the room, yawned, and put her hand over her mouth.

"Sorry."

"I'm right there with you, Bell. I'll be unconscious a minute after I hit the pillow."

The restaurant had dusted the burgers and fries with an extra heap of salt. Bell wished for a jug of water to wash the food down.

"So," Gardy said as he crumpled the food containers and stuffed them into the bag. "You feel okay being back in the field so soon after God's Hand?"

The line of discussion would lead elsewhere, Bell guessed.

"Better than locking myself in my apartment. I've done enough of that."

Indeed, she'd undergone a prolonged psychological evaluation and spent the better part of a year looking over her shoulder for Logan Wolf. After Wolf abducted her during the God's Hand case, she became convinced he was innocent of his wife's murder. Her suspicion someone set up Wolf only grew after a sniper tried to kill them both on a Virginia hillside.

"Talked to Marcel about the missing dogs."

"And?"

Gardy gave a noncommittal nod.

"He's going back through the reports and checking to see if they cluster."

"He should have one of the deputies phone the families. Try to find a common link."

Gardy palmed a handful of fries and chased it down with soda. He stared at Bell as he chewed. Bell set down her burger.

"What?"

Gardy took another sip of soda. The casual way Gardy leaned back in his chair belied the interrogation in his eyes.

"Weber's ready to close the book on the sniper shooting."

This didn't surprise her. Deputy Director Weber rarely saw eye-to-eye with Bell and went out of his way to make her job difficult. But burying his head in the sand after someone attempted to shoot her rattled Bell.

"Tell me something I don't know. Shocking he failed to identify the shooter."

"Let's not twist this into a conspiracy. See things from his perspective."

"Which is?"

Gardy sighed.

"No shells recovered on the hill, no blood. Without a dead body, what does Weber have to go on?"

"I killed him, Gardy. He wore a pendant."

"Marking him as special ops. Yes, I remember."

"You think I concocted the story?"

"No, but I fail to see why you drove there alone in the first place."

"I told you. Congresswoman San Giovanni received a phone call from a man claiming to be God's Hand. The man said he held her daughter at those coordinates, and if anyone besides me showed up, he'd murder the girl."

Gardy bit the inside of his cheek. Bell's decision broke protocol. Before he could launch into another long-winded critique, she steered the conversation back to Shelly LaFleur's murder.

"Let's talk about our unknown subject. We know he's a large man because he perched her up as a scarecrow. Impossible to link the missing dogs yet, but he likely started killing animals. Either way—"

"How about we talk about Logan Wolf?"

Caught off guard, Bell sat back in her chair.

"Okay. Anything in particular?"

"Don't play games, Bell. I can't prove anything, but I'm certain you had contact with Wolf on the night you killed God's Hand."

"You're right, you don't have proof."

"There's a three-hour window when no one can vouch for your location, and somehow you left your apartment without Agent Flanagan's knowledge. It's like you fell off the map. Bell, if Wolf attempted to kidnap you again, there's no reason to hide it from me."

"If Wolf kidnapped me, how did I take down God's Hand?"

Gardy picked at a pile of onion rings, the last of the food.

"In the past, he let you go. Like when he abducted you in Kansas with that insane request."

"He wanted me to profile his wife's killer."

"That's a laugh. You could have held up a mirror."

Gardy turned the box of onion rings toward Bell. She shook her head. As she absently tore at her napkin, he leaned forward.

"You actually believe Wolf, don't you?" She lifted her tired eyes to his. He slapped his palm against his forehead. "No, Bell. I've let you go down a hundred dangerous roads in the past because I trusted your judgment, but not this time."

Here we go again. First Marcel wanted to hide the murder scene from Bell as if she were too brittle to handle the gore. Now Gardy discredited her judgment.

"Don't play parent with me, Gardy."

"I'm the senior agent on this investigation."

"There's no reason to pull rank, and Wolf has nothing to do with this case."

"Strange how you defend him. I'd almost believe you've come to trust the man. Logan Wolf is a master of manipulation and a liar. And a serial killer, in case you've forgotten."

"Wolf doesn't fit the killer's profile."

Gardy laughed and tossed a crumpled napkin into the trash.

"Oh, this should be good."

"You can't explain why he murdered his wife and switched to killing men. Can you?"

"Gee, I don't know. Because he's a psycho, and that's what psychos do?"

"Stop oversimplifying. If this was anyone except Wolf, you'd question the profile."

"But I *know* Wolf. If there's anyone capable of pulling

the wool over your eyes, it's him. He concealed his darkness for years. None of us had a clue. You think it doesn't tear me apart that I worked beside the man and never recognized how dangerous he is? Stop the bullshit. Why are you protecting him?"

"I'm not protecting anyone, but I'm open-minded enough to consider the possibility someone set Wolf up."

"Why would someone set up Logan Wolf?"

"Wolf was in line to become Deputy Director. Maybe somebody wanted him out of the way."

Gardy leaned his head back and laughed.

"You can't be serious. Are you suggesting Don Weber murdered Renee Wolf, planted evidence, and masterminded an agency-wide conspiracy because he wanted the promotion?"

Bell took a deep breath to keep from screaming. Gardy wiped his hands and tossed the last of the food into the trash.

"Listen to what you're saying, Bell. Don Weber doesn't get his nails dirty unless he's picking a golf ball out of the sand at Eastwood Pines. I might despise the guy, but this is the last man on the planet who'd slit a woman's throat and place a sack over her head. He doesn't do the dirty work."

"What if he outsourced?"

Gardy pounded the table. Bell jumped.

"This isn't an X-Files conspiracy. Go around claiming one of the most powerful men in the FBI is a murderer, and you'll end up with a lot worse than a pink slip. Logan Wolf isn't some reclamation project. He's a cold-blooded killer. The next time he comes for you, you won't be so lucky. Don't trust him, Bell."

"That's it," Bell said, standing up and shoving her chair back. "This isn't you, Gardy. You're tired, I'm tired. I'm taking a walk, then I'm heading to bed."

"A walk? You think that's safe?"

"I'm an FBI agent, and I'm packing a Glock."

"This discussion isn't over."

"It is for tonight."

Gardy leaped from his chair when she grabbed the doorknob.

"Come on, Bell." She halted as he ran his hand through his hair. "Look, I'm sorry. Don't leave angry. You need to understand I'm responsible for your safety."

"Don't worry about me, Gardy. I can handle myself. I'd hate for you to get in trouble with the boss if I broke a nail or caught a chill." She glanced around the room and sniffed. "And in here, that wouldn't be difficult."

Bell slammed the door on her way out. Another sleepless night awaited her.

CHAPTER FIVE

Running at the break of dawn often left Clarissa Scott exhausted during the school day, but she had to run now or she'd find an excuse not to exercise after work. Her sandy brown hair tied in a ponytail, Scott jogged out of her house a little after five o'clock, the sun little more than a promise below the hills as stars melted into cobalt blues. From the center of the village, she could see the brick facade of the Golden central school looming over the homes. A little after eight, she'd have a homeroom of fourteen third-graders chattering about video games. The seven-hour day of teaching concluded with bus duty at three. By the time she walked home, her feet would be sore, voice hoarse, and her head achy. Running would be the last thing on her mind.

Clarissa's Nikes slapped the sidewalk as she passed the general store and turned the corner toward Monument Park. Fog concealed the park, the skeletal tops of the slide and swing set poking out of the mist. In any other town, she'd have passed a neighbor or waved to someone driving for an early morning coffee. Not in Golden. With barely enough residents to justify the outdated school and the dozen or so Ma and Pa stores, half of which closed years ago, Clarissa was more likely to run past a deer or raccoon than another human.

Yet there was another person in the fog. Idling in a van outside the park. In another minute, she'd jog past the vehicle, a long, white van with black lettering etched in cursive across the doors. A landscaping van, she thought, though it was impossible to read from this distance. For now, the van rumbled curbside in a low growl, agitating the mist.

Uneasy, Clarissa crossed the street to run down the opposite sidewalk. News around town claimed someone murdered a farmer on the outskirts of Golden. The sheriff's department provided sketchy details, doing their best to keep the Syracuse and Watertown media at bay, yet rumors swirled around a ritualistic killing and a potential serial killer loose in the countryside. Clarissa believed neither rumor and chalked them up to inebriated banter over beers at Steven's Pub. But logic didn't prevent her heart from quickening when the van's brake lights flared like angry eyes in the fog. Like demon eyes.

A line of old two-story homes bordered the sidewalk, windows dark, no evidence of life inside. She tripped on a rolled newspaper haphazardly tossed across the sidewalk and fell down on all fours, certain she'd injured her ankle. Wincing, she slid her hand across her knees and felt blood. Great. This is what she got for running blind. But it was the shearing pain in her ankle that shocked her, and as she lay clutching her leg, moaning with the crumbling sidewalk digging into her side, the fear she'd injured herself and couldn't struggle back to the center of town sent her into a panic.

She wasn't aware the van sat across the road until a door clicked open. Then the metallic whirl of a sliding door.

Footsteps clonked the pavement. Coming closer.

Clarissa pushed herself up, legs trembling while she braced her arm against a tree.

Then a loud slap against the macadam as the driver unloaded a heavy bag and tossed it down. Then another. At least she thought they were bags and not dead bodies. Next, he dragged the bags…or bodies…over the curb and toward the shadows of the baseball dugout. She pictured a bloody corpse, the man gripping his prey by the hair. Dragging his quarry into the gloom.

She edged back from the curb and threw a glance over her shoulder at the porch steps. If the man came after her, she'd clamber up the stairs and pound on the door.

It was quiet now, no indication of where the man hid in the fog.

"Hello? Someone there?"

His voice came from the park near the dugout. He couldn't see her, but maybe he discerned her sneakers scraping the pavement when she crept toward the steps.

He lumbered in heavy work boots out of the park, swished through the grass. Heading right for her.

The warped stairs squealed and gave her away when she stepped down. He came faster now, footfalls thumping against the street and zeroing in on her.

But as his silhouette materialized in the fog, a hand clutched her mouth from behind. She screamed into the palm, smelling sweat and an earthy scent. A forearm snaked around her neck and squeezed, her sneakers sliding uselessly against the wood slats as the figure pulled her back from the stairs and behind a shrub.

The last thing she heard was a door slam before the van pulled off the curb. She lost consciousness as the first ray from the sun sliced a hole in the mist.

CHAPTER SIX

The sheriff phoned Gardy a few minutes before noon. Paging through the case notes in the rental parked outside LaFleur's farmhouse, Bell looked up when Gardy's voice altered from casual to concerned.

"How long has she been missing?"

A pause.

Bell mouthed, "What's happening?"

Gardy waved her question away and swung the phone to his opposite ear as he engaged the engine. He activated the GPS and pulled up a map of Golden, just a few lines converging on a small grid of streets in the center of town.

"Four hours isn't a long time, Sheriff…uh-huh…right. Okay, we'll meet you outside the house in ten minutes."

Gardy jammed the phone into his pocket and reversed the vehicle. The tires kicked up a storm of dust as he executed a hurried three-point turn, then they hurtled down the dirt road toward Golden.

"You plan to tell me what's up, or am I still persona non grata?"

Hands clasped to the wheel, Gardy glanced across the seat.

"That was Marcel. A third-grade teacher, Clarissa Scott, didn't show up for school today, and she isn't answering her door."

Bell did the math in her head.

"They declared her missing after four hours?"

"That was my reaction, but the school insists she's the last person to skip out on her kids. And with a killer roaming the area..."

"They're not taking any chances. Okay, got it."

The brief exchange represented the breadth of their conversation since meeting outside the motel at eight. Gardy offered a curt nod before refocusing on the road, a not-so-subtle hint the small talk had run its course. The remainder of the trip, Gardy remained aloof, his jaw set in an irritated clench.

"Here we are," he said before slamming the shifter into park. He exited the vehicle without another word.

Bell sighed and gathered her bag. The rental stood outside a red ranch house with a brick walkway to the door and a pot of flowers beneath the mailbox. A wooden sign hanging above the door offered welcome, though Bell wondered how many visitors Scott received in such a small village.

Sheriff Marcel touched the brim of his hat as Bell approached. She didn't know how to take the gesture. Normally it would have seemed polite, a measure of respect for another law enforcement officer, but coming from Marcel the gesture felt hackneyed and trite, a nod a man reserved for his mother.

After Marcel briefed the agents, Gardy decided they

should split, Bell canvassing the neighborhood with one of the deputies, Gardy heading back to the sheriff's office to coordinate with Harold at the BAU. Craving a break from Gardy, Bell agreed. Until Marcel, himself, opted to partner with her.

The sheriff wore a grave expression as they knocked on doors, barely glancing in Bell's direction as he led the way. An elderly man two doors from Scott's home mentioned the teacher liked to run before school.

"Did you see Ms Scott this morning?" Marcel asked.

The man brushed at his white mustache.

"Yes, but it's not like I spy on my neighbors. She's a jogger, that one. Likes to run through the village and circle back. She's usually dressed and headed out the door by seven, but not today. Made me wonder what happened to her."

For a man who didn't spy on his neighbors, he seemed to know Scott's schedule down to the minute.

"Did you call anyone when she didn't return?"

"I don't poke my nose into people's business."

"Okay. Any idea where she likes to run?"

"Down to Monument Park. Seems dangerous for a woman to be out on her own like that before the sun rises, but I don't pry."

The other neighbors told similar stories. Clarissa Scott seemed like a nice enough lady, someone to exchange pleasantries with now-and-then, but nobody knew her. The Golden townsfolk were old-timers, born and raised in this little village. Scott was an outsider, and that's all she'd ever be to them.

Marcel's truck puffed sunbaked heat when they climbed inside. Bell wished the sheriff would roll the windows down. Instead, he set the temperature control at 72. Predictably, it took ages for the air conditioner to kick in. He pointed the truck toward the village center while Bell gazed out the window, picturing the most likely route Scott took each morning. The misshapen sidewalk flexed and ramped, repaving long overdue, but it wasn't a problem for an experienced runner. Behind them, a county route meandered into the wilderness. Bell, who liked to run along the beach outside her Chesapeake Bay apartment, figured she'd jog the county route as a change of pace on the weekend, but Scott would want to stay close to home weekdays so she wasn't late for school.

"Turn here," Bell said when they reached the corner.

"But the stores are in the other direction."

"And they wouldn't be open at the break of dawn. Besides, she wants scenery when she runs, and abandoned storefronts don't fit the bill."

Marcel thought for a second, nodded, and wheeled the truck to the right.

"Now where?"

Leaning forward, sensing Scott's trail, Bell scanned the possible routes. The way ahead cut between a scattering of ramshackle homes. A baseball field lay to the left—Monument Park, she guessed—and a few well-constructed old homes stood across the street.

"Toward the park."

She opted against explaining her sixth sense for tracking victims and murderers, figuring Marcel would respect her methods as much as he would an astrologist's or clairvoyant's. He tapped the steering wheel to a country song and watched her from the corner of his eye.

"So you're rather famous, I gather."

Wonderful. Another reader of *The Informer*, the tabloid obsessed with serial killers and the sexy FBI agent who hunts them. Their words, not hers. Lacking an appropriate response, she let the comment hang until he spoke again.

"Caught that monster down in Coral Lake last year. Not sure why Sheriff Lerner went straight to the FBI when he could have called us in to help." Bell clamped her tongue against the roof of her mouth and let him continue. "Then again, Lerner's a politician, not a cop. Guy couldn't catch a raccoon pillaging his garbage."

Bell snorted. She wasn't about to badmouth Lerner in front of the neighboring county's sheriff, but Marcel hit the nail on the head. After she captured and killed Alan Hodge, Lerner stabbed the agents in the back and vied for the spotlight, claiming Gardy and Bell intruded on his investigation.

"Yeah, you're quite the celebrity."

Celebrity rolled off his tongue with distaste.

"Not by my own choice."

"No?" He glanced at her, then back at the road, the baseball field rolling out in summery greens fifty feet ahead. "So all that stuff they wrote about you taking down the God's Hand killer single-handedly were lies?"

Bell clenched her hands.

"I was alone. I took a dangerous man out of the world and made certain an abducted girl made it back to her mother. Not once did I consider my popularity. What would you have done?"

Marcel, an imposing figure were it not for the uniform and kindly face, glared down at her from beneath his hat. Bell recognized the look. It was the same one her father afforded a younger Bell when she'd done wrong.

"I would have waited for backup, not rushed in like Stallone in a bad Rambo sequel. You keep driving with the pedal mashed to the floor, and sooner or later you'll take the car over a cliff."

Bell opened her mouth and shut it. The argument wasn't winnable, not worth the aggravation. Steam blew from her ears as the truck passed the park.

"Stop the truck."

"Here?"

"Pull over."

She'd already forgotten Marcel reading her the riot act when she hopped out of the cab.

"Hold up, Agent Bell," he said, but she jumped the curb and pressed herself against the chain-link fence.

Despite the noon sun, darkness billowed out from the dugout, the ceiling and walls a shield against the daylight. Her heart raced as she considered the possibilities. Scott jogging past the park and hearing something in the dugout. A cry for help, perhaps. No, the scenario didn't feel right. But she was close. The killer took Scott nearby.

She wheeled around and assessed the surroundings. Marcel waddled up to her, a slight limp she hadn't noticed before.

"Leg cramps up on me when I don't stretch it enough. Don't grow old, Agent Bell." He winced and followed her vision. "Why did we stop?"

"There." She focused on a white streak near the curb. Bending down, she scooped the powder into her hand and sniffed it. "Chalk?"

"Sure. The youth league teams start practice this week, so it's time to reline the fields. Not sure how they do it in Golden, but in my hometown, a crew member drops the bags off first thing in the morning, and they line the fields after the dew dries up."

Bell stood and surveyed the sky.

"Sheriff, did it rain last night?"

"No, ma'am. Rained yesterday morning."

"So it stands to reason someone dropped the bags off this morning, otherwise, the rain would have washed it away yesterday."

"I guess."

"Who makes the deliveries?"

Marcel shrugged.

"Local parks personnel? I can check around."

As though she hadn't heard, Bell followed the curb. A muddy tire track curled into the road and vanished before the corner. She photographed the tracks as Marcel came to her side, itching his head.

"Seems like a wild goose chase, Agent Bell."

"How do you mean?"

"Those tracks could be from anyone. Even if the deliveryman left them, doesn't mean he abducted Clarissa Scott. Heck, we don't even know if she came this way today."

Bell thumbed through the photographs and verified the images were crisp and clear.

"She came this way, Sheriff, like the neighbor said. I would have. Not many route choices in Golden."

"I suppose," Marcel said, unconvinced.

Across the street, the sidewalk crumbled in a deep state of disrepair. A pair of homes stood to either side. Wooden steps climbing up to the entryway of a white two-story drew her attention, though she couldn't say why.

"We're not getting anywhere," Marcel said, removing his hat and fanning his sweat-beaded face. "Best we head over to the school, don't you think?"

No, nobody at the school could tell them where Clarissa Scott disappeared to. But Marcel was insistent, and Bell climbed into the truck, sensing she'd lost Scott's trail.

CHAPTER SEVEN

As Bell presumed, Golden Central School turned out to be a dead end. Except for the dogged insistence by everyone from the principal down to the janitorial staff that Clarissa Scott loved her job and wouldn't abandon her kids, nobody offered an explanation for her disappearance. By all accounts Scott was a beloved member of the school, though the community treated her like a ghost. Like all teachers, she butted heads with faculty members, and Scott and Mrs Erst, the fourth grade science teacher, had a running dispute over teaching methods, but Erst was sixty-three, a hair over five foot, and walked with a cane. Not a likely suspect to overpower Scott and throw her in the back of a truck.

Bell and Gardy reconvened at the County Sheriff's office, a squat brick-and-mortar building with an American flag flying above a landscaped walkway. Through the break room window, Bell spied the blue shingles of the County Corner's Building. An unwelcome vision of Shelly LaFleur's pallid body came to her. What little information they had to work with suggested the killer kept LaFleur alive for two or three days before he murdered her, and that was based on nebulous accounts by witnesses who claimed they *might* have seen LaFleur in the village square earlier in the week.

Bell and Gardy exchanged only a few words, Gardy grunting instead of replying to Bell's questions. The intolerable conversation ended when a large, forty-something man wearing a gray Golden Parks t-shirt entered the sheriff's department with Deputy Rasovich.

Gardy glanced up.

"That Drake Quentin?"

"Must be. Marcel works fast. I'll give him that."

Earlier, Marcel phoned the parks department and spoke to Quentin, the man who'd delivered a bag of chalk and several wheelbarrow loads of soil to the field that morning. When Marcel mentioned the missing jogger, Quentin went quiet for a moment, then admitted a woman was in the fog.

The square interrogation room stretched a little longer than a postage stamp, and it took considerable effort for Marcel, Bell, and Gardy to wiggle into chairs across the scratched wooden table from Quentin. Quentin fiddled with his hands, eyes darting around the room.

Marcel chose the agents to lead the questioning, and Gardy deferred to Bell who'd become the de facto interrogator during the short time they partnered together. While Marcel leaned back in his chair, glare fixed on Quentin, Bell removed a notepad and began the interview.

"How long have you worked for Golden Parks, Mr Quentin?"

"Since summer of 1996."

Quentin's voice quivered, and he swallowed after

answering.

"Summer of 1996? That's a long time. Have you lived in Golden your entire life?"

Bell had already learned the answer from Marcel. She wanted to get Quentin talking, establish trust.

"Yes."

"College?"

"No. Never saw much need for that."

"What made you want to work for the parks? Do you like being around children?"

Quentin's spine straightened as he glanced between the faces across the table.

"Now, hold on. You're trying to make it sound like I'm a sicko or something."

"Not at all, Mr Quentin. I want to understand why you chose your line of work."

He shrugged.

"I grew up playing ball on the town field. Cleanup hitter for Golden High in 1993, seven home runs my senior year." Quentin smiled at the memory. The grin faded when nobody reciprocated from the other side of the table. "Anyhow, I knew a little about how to keep the field in shape. Seemed like an easy job, unloading and loading supplies, drawing the chalk lines on a summer morning with no supervisor breathing down my neck."

"Sounds like relaxing work."

"It is except when you get a rainy summer like last year. Then you can't keep up with the mowing, and the infield turns into a swamp. You have to fill the holes and rake the field so it's smooth. Don't want somebody's kid tearing up his knee on account of your negligence. Besides, Golden is a small town. Everyone knows everyone. We all look out for each other."

Bell smiled.

"Did you deliver supplies to the baseball field on Oak Street early this morning?"

"Yes. Chalk and soil, just like I told the sheriff."

"You told Sheriff Marcel you heard a woman across the street. Is that accurate?"

"I *th*ink so. It sounded like she fell. You need to understand the fog was so damn thick I couldn't find the fence gate."

Bell narrowed her eyes and clicked the pen.

"Let me get this straight. A strong, good-looking man like yourself hears an injured woman, and he doesn't cross the street to help?"

Quentin gave Marcel a pleading stare before turning back to Bell.

"Listen, I'm not positive of anything. There was a sound like someone tripped, and then a voice. I called out to whoever it was. Three, four times, and nobody answered. So someone fell on the sidewalk. What's this about, anyway?"

Marcel handed Bell a staff photograph of Clarissa Scott. She passed it across the table to Quentin. Bell watched for his reaction.

"Do you recognize this woman?"

Quentin picked up the picture, his thumb and forefinger holding the photograph at the corner. He tilted it.

"Yeah, I see her around. She's a runner. Snow or rain, she's out there first thing every morning." Reality dawned on his face. "Wait, you don't think I did anything to her, do you?"

"You're not a suspect," Bell said, though Quentin was their best lead.

"Was it her? The woman in the fog?"

"That's what we're trying to find out. Her name is Clarissa Scott. She teaches third grade."

"Gee, I hope nothing bad happened to her. Hey, this isn't related to that murdered farmer, is it?"

"I never said it was, Mr Quentin. Consider this an information gathering session." Quentin nodded, but Bell noted the way he squirmed in his chair. "Did you know Shelly LaFleur?"

"Sure." Quentin waved his hands when Bell wrote on her notepad. "What I mean is I saw her in town at the general store and every Saturday at market, but I didn't *know her* know her."

"You're an intelligent man, Mr Quentin. Do you own a computer?"

"Why does it matter?"

"Please answer the question."

"Yeah. It's not a crime."

"Do you have a website?"

"I have a Facebook if that's what you mean. Never use it, though. I thought this was about an injured woman?"

Bell glanced at Gardy, and he shook his head. Quentin couldn't tell a server from a broccoli plant.

The man's brow beaded sweat. Marcel dug a handkerchief from his jacket and offered it to Quentin.

"No, I'm fine."

Bell set her pen down.

"You seem nervous, Mr Quentin."

"No...I, uh...well, you'd be nervous if two FBI agents

and the county sheriff claimed you'd hurt someone."

"Calm down. Take a deep breath." Bell waited until Quentin composed himself. "Let's talk about Scott and LaFleur. You ever see them together?"

Quentin itched his head.

"Not that I can remember."

"Can you think why anyone would want to hurt them?"

"In Golden? No way. You ask me, the people who killed the farmer lady came from Syracuse. Nothing but criminals in that city."

"So a group of people murdered LaFleur."

Quentin lowered his eyes to the table.

"Could be. I'm not sure. But Golden is full of good people, not murderers."

"Something confuses me. Earlier you claimed everyone in Golden knows each other, and you look out for your neighbors."

"We do."

"Yet I mentioned Shelly LaFleur and Clarissa Scott, one murdered, the other missing and potentially injured, and you don't speak to either. And you care for each other, but if you spot an injured woman across the street, you leave her alone in the fog and drive off."

Wiping his brow on his t-shirt, Quentin sniffled, eyes watery.

"I don't know everyone, okay? Sometimes people move to Golden and they don't run in your circle. Besides, I figured the woman was fine because she left around the back of the house. I figured if she walked, she was okay, or maybe it was the woman who lives there picking up the newspaper. I might have misheard."

Bell pictured the house across from the park.

"The white two-story with the big porch?"

"Yeah…I mean, I guess. I couldn't see."

Bell caught Gardy's eye. He nodded at her to wrap up the interview.

After Quentin departed the station, Gardy pulled Bell aside in the break room.

"You think he's our guy?" Gardy asked, lowering his voice when Deputy Greene sauntered to the coffee pot.

Tempted to lay into Gardy for giving her the cold shoulder all day, Bell took a composing breath.

"No. He's the right size, and I don't buy the bullshit about painting Golden like Mayberry, but he didn't do this."

"How can you be sure?"

"The guy we're looking for is mentally ill. The crown of thorns suggests a religious aspect not unlike God's Hand. Quentin doesn't possess any of those traits."

"That's reasonable."

"It's not a shot in the dark that he heard Scott in the fog. She's the only person in town running the sidewalks at that time of morning."

Greene filled his cup slowly, probably listening in. Gardy folded his arms and leaned against the counter until the junior deputy moved on.

"A little obvious on the eavesdropping," Gardy said, reaching for a Styrofoam cup as he cocked his head at the departing deputy. "Take Marcel back to Oak Street. I'll call Harold and have him check Quentin's background, make sure we didn't miss anything."

Bell cringed at the thought of another investigation with the sheriff. Before she could protest, Gardy grabbed his coffee and left her alone in the break room.

CHAPTER EIGHT

The dream dims, and she no longer stands before the children, the classroom vanished.

She blinks several times before the double vision clears. Her neck aches, and swallowing burns the back of her throat.

A confused scene surrounds her. Unlaundered clothing strewn about a tattered rug. Wood-paneled walls, circa 1975. Half-light borne of hazy sunshine through gray, translucent drapes as though day and night vie for supremacy before her.

Footsteps overhead jolt her awake. Clarissa Scott remembers running in the mist. Falling. A man yelling to her before a hand reached out of the darkness and cupped her mouth. Someone abducted her. Who?

Yet no one guards Scott. No ropes bind her. Daylight beckons, urges her to flee while she has the opportunity.

The ceiling groans. She struggles to her feet and crosses the room. Sees a green-tiled hallway. Muddy footprints track to-and-from the room.

Back to the wall, she slides along the hall. Past a

kitchen with a dripping faucet. *Plunk, plunk, plunk,* then a louder creak above her head.

She continues down the hall. An empty room stands to the left. The stairway to the second floor climbs straight ahead. To the right, a foyer with an empty coat rack is tucked into the corner.

And a door.

Her heart pounds. It seems too easy.

Scott edges past the coat rack. Freezes when the hangers rock. Fate is on her side when the hangers don't clang together.

Something is wrong with the doorknob. What is out of place? No button. The knob requires a key to unlock.

Frenzied, she yanks on the door. Twists the knob against the locking mechanism. It won't budge. Scott pulls harder as though she can muscle her way to freedom.

A narrow rectangular window accepts a shaft of light. If she breaks the glass, he will hear, and undoubtedly the door won't open from the outside without a key.

Swallowing a sob, she retraces her steps and peeks inside the empty room. This was once a bedroom, she thinks. Scrapes mar the bare wood where someone dragged furniture across the floor. Bars cover the windows.

Again, the ceiling protests under the man's weight. He is at the top of the stairs. Listening for her.

She backtracks to the kitchen and searches for another door.

Now the stairs creak under the weight of a large, strong body. She scurries back to the room she awoke in, a trapped rat, as the footsteps come closer.

Scott searches for something to defend herself with. Considers the lamp but knows it will be ineffective. His shadow grows along the wall before she sees him, and she envisions a nightmare monster shuffling down the hall.

When he turns the corner, she sees he isn't demon or monster, but an ordinary looking man with no discernible facial features except for the eyes, which appear slightly offset, the left socket a fraction higher than the right.

He wears a red flannel shirt, blue jeans tucked into work boots, and a baseball cap over a nest of curly, brown hair. Somehow his normalcy frightens her more than a monster would, for she cannot believe one of her neighbors, a man she might have passed on the street, abducts women. The light catches him in side profile, and she realizes she's seen him before. Where? His facial features and shy mannerisms are familiar. Every time Scott tries to recall, the memory slips through her fingers, lost in a whirlpool between her aching head and pure terror.

Despite his placid appearance, hostile energy surrounds him. Volatility.

"Are you cold?"

She doesn't understand why the man would ask her such a thing until she realizes she's trembling. When she doesn't answer, he kneels before her, studies her the way one would a sick pet. While he glares, she discerns a strange sound in the distance. A constant *whump whump whump* repeating every few seconds. As she recognizes her abductor, she also finds the noise familiar. Attentive to the sound, she almost places it before he speaks and breaks her concentration.

"As I told you, no reason exists for your terror." Her skin creeps with the possibility he'd spoken to her while she slept. Leered over her. "Sin is a badge all of us wear. We're imperfect, flawed. Would you like something to drink? You must be thirsty."

His eyes light as though he'd invited her into his home for tea and cookies.

Scott's voice dies before she can say, "no," and she shakes her head as he glares at her.

Disconnected. That is the impression he gives her. As if two different men breathe behind his eyes. One kindly, the other insane.

Her attention drifts around the room, possibly a den, as he speaks. So many items look out of place in the den. On the wall is a cross chained to a string of rosary beads. Inconsistent with the wood paneling, a modern lamp with an LED fixture stands in the corner. The chair, couch, and end tables appear mismatched, the furniture cobbled together from garage sales or low-end consignment stores. And a jumbled mess of sticks and twine spill off an end table.

No, not sticks. Prickers. Thorns.

Her eyes widen on the thorns, though she cannot say why. Swallowing, she finds her voice.

"Why did you bring me here?"

He crosses the room to the end table. Hunches over. Runs his hands along the thorns.

"Please, just let me go," she says, crawling into the corner and drawing her knees to her chest. "I won't tell anyone. I swear."

The man doesn't notice or doesn't care, so enraptured is he with the thorns. His gaze moves to Scott, and a shiver ripples through her body.

"It wasn't me she wanted," he goes on as if she hadn't spoken. "I thought it was at the time, but we are all imperfect. Who am I to pretend I am without flaw? Those were different days, though. No cell phones, no Internet. We played outside all day, and when our parents called us in at night, nobody locked their doors. We trusted. Maybe not strangers. You always had to be careful with them. But people we knew..."

Like a phantom, he floats out of the room without finishing his thought. Beyond the wall comes the sound of running water. The clink of a glass set upon the counter.

Her chin falls to her chest. Dark hair unravels and cloaks her face.

She looks down and sees the blood spots in the carpet. Not an arterial spray, but a scattering of droplets crust the fibers together.

Scott screams, and no hero comes to save her.

CHAPTER NINE

Sheriff Marcel intimated his belief they'd wasted time with Drake Quentin as he escorted Bell back to Golden and along Oak Street.

"Is this one of those *visions* profilers get?"

Bell rubbed at her eyes.

"No visions, Sheriff. Just hunches based on evidence and logical conclusions."

"Evidence," Marcel huffed over a snicker. "We're chasing after rainbows for a pot of gold."

Bell ignored the comment.

"Anything on the missing dogs cases?"

Marcel nodded and rubbed at his chin.

"Now that's something worth pursuing. I sent Rasovich and Monteville out to interview the families again. Five households altogether. Is it the same guy?"

"Wouldn't be the first time a budding murderer cut his teeth with animals. But this isn't an ordinary killer. He's bouncing his website through multiple dark web servers. Taunting us, really."

Marcel's fingers tightened on the wheel.

The baseball field had a fresh look to it when they neared the park, the lines bright and striking against a green only seen during a rainy season, and it had poured for much of the last month.

Greasy black hair, dressed in a navy blue sweat suit, Reginald Schultz opened the door so quickly Bell figured he'd spied them through the window from the moment the big truck pulled curbside.

Marcel flashed his badge.

"Mr Schultz?"

In his mid-sixties, Schultz regarded the badge over his glasses as though he doubted its authenticity.

"Yes? Who wants to know?"

"I'm Sheriff Marcel, and this is Agent Bell with the FBI."

Schultz raised an eyebrow.

"FBI? What's she doing here?"

"Sir," Bell said, sliding her badge into her pocket. "Did you notice a woman outside your apartment between five and six this morning? She may have injured herself."

"Wasn't up that early. How she get injured?"

"We're looking into that. She's a jogger, and it's possible she didn't see the buckled sidewalk with the fog being so thick."

For a moment, Bell felt certain Schultz would spit.

"Been telling the village they need to fix that sidewalk for over ten years, and you think they listen? Someone was bound to get hurt." His eyes narrowed. "You best not be considering a lawsuit. That sidewalk is the village's responsibility. I got a good lawyer."

"Nobody's blaming you, Mr Shultz," Marcel said, waving his hands in appeasement.

"Sure, you say that now, then the woman decides she wants money and the village attorney sends me a notice. I know how this works. Someone's always looking to sue these days. I complained to your office last summer about the damn kids tracking across my yard. Just a matter of time before one of them falls and takes me to court."

"You called our office?"

"That's what I get living across the street from a park. They trudge through with their bats and gloves like my property is the only path to the field. I tell 'em, 'use the damn sidewalk. This ain't a highway.' But they keep coming. Walked through my garden this morning, they did. Right over the lettuce and chard. Damn vagrants."

Bell locked eyes with Marcel. She knew what he was thinking. School was in session this morning. Kids wouldn't head to the park at sunrise.

"Mr Schultz," Bell said. "Could you show us the footprints?"

Schultz grinned.

"Certainly. It's about time you caught those hoodlums."

Bell and Marcel followed as Schultz marched them around the house, past trellised grapevines curling up the side, then to a tilled garden. Various greens grew out of mounds at regular, almost military-perfect spacing.

"See what I mean?" Schultz knelt beside a crushed lettuce plant, lifting its leaves as if he meant to resuscitate the lettuce. "Walked through the garden without a care."

Bell bent to examine the prints. Marcel placed his foot beside the print to compare.

"Awfully big for a kid," Marcel said. "Looks like an adult, if you ask me."

"Nah, it's kids. I watch 'em through the back window. They don't care about nothin' but themselves."

Bell photographed the footprint. A broken line ran parallel through the dirt, and Bell pictured the heel of Scott's sneaker digging through the soil as someone dragged her away.

"That look like he pulled Scott along?"

Marcel glared at the pattern, then shook his head.

"It's possible. That mark could be anything."

Rising, she cupped a hand over her eyes to block out the sun and considered the prints. They arrowed toward a stand of trees.

"Figure out who did this?" Schultz asked Bell, interjecting himself into the investigation.

"What's on the other side of those trees?"

Schultz shrugged.

"Riverside Place and the old corset factory. Nothing else. Don't know what they'd want with an abandoned factory, but you can't figure kids these days."

Marcel opened his wallet and handed his card to Schultz.

"If you remember anything else, don't hesitate to call."

Schultz's eyes widened.

"That's it? I lost half my crop."

He continued to yell as Bell and Marcel stepped through the garden, careful not to tread upon the plants.

Marcel removed his hat and wiped his forehead.

"So your working theory is the unknown subject grabbed Scott, then escaped through Schultz's backyard with the fog as cover and headed toward Riverside."

"It's the only thing we have to go on. Did you just call

him an unknown subject?"

Marcel's mouth curled into a smile, the first instance he'd regarded her without animosity today.

"I know a little jargon. Either that or I'm addicted to too many TV shows." A pricker bush blocked the pathway to Riverside. Marcel held the thorns aside for Bell. "What made you want to work for the BAU? A lot of darkness in that line of work."

Bell gave him a guarded look.

"You mean you didn't read *The Informer* articles?"

"Skimmed them. Figured I ought to learn more about Agent Bell after the Coral Lake murders, but I didn't want to wade through the muck to get answers."

Though Bell wished to put the God's Hand memory behind her, she retold the story of the serial killer who murdered her childhood friend and attempted to abduct Bell. By the time she finished, they'd reached the Riverside curb.

Marcel regarded Bell with a tight-lipped grimace, but he didn't reply.

As Schultz told them, an abandoned factory slumbered across the street, half the windows boarded or missing, the black holes like empty eyes peering over a parking lot of broken glass and garbage. Plywood boarded the doors from entry, and the windows were too far off the ground to lift a body through.

"So if someone kidnapped Scott across the street from the park, and that's a big if," Marcel said, hands on hips as he surveyed the street, "he'd need a getaway vehicle. Fog or no fog, you don't drag a screaming woman for a block without someone reporting a commotion."

Bell swiveled around and lined up the path from the

garden to the street.

"If he parked along Piper, we should check with the neighbors."

One lone house, a red ranch with black shutters, stood across from the factory.

"You want to do the honors this time?"

Bell led Marcel up the porch steps. She pressed the doorbell, and it rang deep inside the home. After nobody responded, she rang again. Thirty seconds passed in uncomfortable silence, but when Marcel cleared his throat, the muffled thuds of footsteps approached the door.

A balding man with glasses and a llama face answered.

"Help ya?"

Bell read the name on the mailbox.

"Mr Ripple?"

"John Ripple, yes."

"Agent Bell, FBI," she said, removing the badge from her pocket. "And this is Sheriff Marcel."

Ripple stepped onto the porch and shut the door behind him.

"FBI, huh? This have anything to do with that farmer?"

"We're investigating a missing persons report. We have reason to believe she was near the park around sunrise this morning." Ripple crossed his arms and leaned over the rail so he could see the park. "Did you see or hear anyone outside your house?"

"No women, but somebody parked a truck outside the house before dawn."

Bell eyed Marcel, who pulled out a pen.

"Can you describe the truck?"

"Black. A big pickup, 4x4 type. Couldn't tell you the make, though. Nothing I recall seeing before."

"You didn't happen to read the license plate, did you?"

Ripple shook his head.

"No reason to. I thought it was odd, someone parking outside the house so early, but I assumed it was one of the park crews."

"And you didn't see the driver?"

"Well, no. I noticed the truck when I got up to make my coffee. By the time I showered, it had gone."

"And what time was that?" Marcel said, glancing between Ripple and his notepad.

"Six, six-thirty. The driver must have driven off while I was in the shower. I would have heard an engine that size, otherwise."

Marcel handed out another card, but Bell didn't expect Ripple to call. On the way back to the sheriff's truck, Marcel kept shooting Bell glances. At first, she surmised Marcel was trawling for another argument, but the sheriff seemed troubled. Even haunted.

"Something on your mind?" Bell asked.

Marcel looked sheepishly at the ground.

"My apologies. It's just that…"

"What?"

"You remind me of someone."

Paging through the interview notes as she walked, Bell giggled.

"You work with a lot of FBI agents who chase gold at the end of rainbows?"

Marcel fumbled through his pockets for the keys.

"Not exactly."

"So who?"

He stopped at the truck, keys in hand, weighing whether he should reply or shut his mouth and unlock the door.

"Juliette Marcel. She was my sister."

The key fob unlocked the doors, and Bell climbed into the passenger seat. *Was* my sister. She chewed on the thought as the sheriff slid behind the wheel, the truck shaking under his girth. The engine rumbled. Marcel pointed them toward the county road which took them to the office.

He remained quiet for many minutes. No music. Only the pop and squawk of the police radio and the rolling hum of the tires. The silence almost made her think wistfully of conversations with Gardy. Almost. For the time being, she celebrated the silence and studied the endless patchwork of forest and meadow sweeping past the window.

When he broke the quiet, she jolted.

"She was only thirty-two." The words pulled her attention. She realized he spoke of his sister. "Good cop. Better than me, that's for sure. Said I was her inspiration." He chuckled without mirth and returned his concentration to the road. "She'd stationed in Rochester back then. Wanted to work her way back home, get away from the city, but I told her to hang in there. Make her mark, do things her way."

The silence returned. Marcel wrestled with a memory.

"A call came into the office. Domestic dispute in a bad part of town. They found the front door open, moths buzzing around the porch light. Juliette knocked. No one answered. Her partner was a rookie, green as algae after a flood. Juliette went in first. They always tell you the first thing you do...the very first thing...is you clear the corner. Your most vulnerable point is the one you can't see."

His mouth opened and clamped shut. The road pulled them forward, a double yellow line slicing past the truck as the first residences announced the next town.

"I'm sorry," Bell said as the station came into view.

Rather than replying, Marcel hit the gas and shot through a yellow light. Bell felt surprised to find herself trembling with pent up emotion when Marcel brought them to a stop beside his deputies' trucks.

She grabbed the door handle but sensed his stare.

"Always check the corners, Agent Bell."

CHAPTER TEN

Bell stepped out of the motel room and into the night. She wondered where Clarissa Scott was and if the woman had seen the land drag the sun down. If she was still alive. No, Bell wouldn't do that to herself. Time remained to rescue the teacher.

Since Gardy's blowup, Bell had felt alone on this case. Outside of a professional capacity, Gardy still wouldn't talk to her, and he'd remained stoic on the drive back to the hotel. Usually he invited her over to eat after work. Tonight, he took his sandwich and she hers, and they entered separate rooms without a word.

The peepers sang loud outside the motel. A silver mist crawled across the meadow and encroached on the road. She glanced around for signs of civilization beyond the motel lot and found none. Walking in the dark seemed like a worse idea by the minute, but she needed to clear her head.

And there was something she'd put off for too long.

After ensuring Gardy wasn't peeking through his curtains, Bell inserted the key and crept into her room. She snatched the holster and gun, concealing both beneath an over-sized sweatshirt. Digging through her bag, she closed her hand over the hidden phone. A moment of paranoia touched her like cold, dead hands in a graveyard. She spun around to an empty room, the curtains cloaking the window, night creeping around the edges.

"You're a little old to believe in monsters," she said to the face in the grimy mirror.

Bell pocketed the phone, one of three burners Logan Wolf had dropped on her kitchen table a week ago—she had no idea how he'd broken into the apartment, for she returned to find the door bolted as she'd left it—and opened the door with one anxious hand touching the Glock through her sweatshirt.

The parking lot appeared darker than it had moments before. She edged the door shut, careful it didn't click and alert Gardy. Then she turned the corner and jogged across the blacktop, casting glances over her shoulder until certain no one followed.

The phone reception improved near the road. A stand of trees provided cover. As she waded through a dew-laden meadow, a motel room door shut behind her. Instinctively, she pulled the gun from her holster and aimed it into the mist. Nobody followed. Probably just Gardy making a run for the vending machine. Feeling stupid, she holstered her weapon and dialed the number Wolf had programmed into the phone. She didn't take note of the number, knowing it was pointless to track him. The serial killer cycled through burners and would dispose of his phone.

The phone rang four times. Bell wondered if Wolf was asleep. Did fugitive murderers sleep? On the fifth ring, the call connected.

Wolf didn't say hello. Quiet followed through the speaker.

"Wolf? You there?"

No reply. Bell cursed the cheap phone. Then the eerie, musical voice of Logan Wolf, a Chopin piece played in a dark and somber key, spoke to her.

"What a pleasant surprise, Agent Bell. I see you located my gifts without issue."

"Get one thing straight, Wolf. You need permission to enter my home."

"Am I a vampire, Scarlett?"

"Don't test me tonight. I'm not in the mood."

Wolf snickered. She'd phoned him because, unlike Gardy, Wolf knew the hillside sniper was real and had taken a bullet in the shoulder the night Bell killed God's Hand. With Weber burying the truth, the serial killer became an unfortunate ally. But what good was Wolf if he played games with her?

"Cheap motel beds and fast food will do that to a body."

Bell lowered the phone and drew herself into the shadows. The silhouette of a silo grew out of the distant horizon, the sky sprinkled with stars.

"Are you following me? Show yourself."

"Easy, Scarlett. Just an elementary deduction. The news claims a murderer is loose in the little village of Golden. What a shame. Northern New York is quite pleasant this time of year. I see only one motel listing in Golden, and it isn't exactly the Four Seasons. Enjoying yourself?"

Wolf followed serial killer activity. One could come to

the obvious conclusion Bell and Gardy were in Golden, but Wolf's guess was too close for comfort. Agitated by the wind, mist swirled through the tall grass and ascended like an angry ghost.

"I'll help you, Scarlett, if you allow. I'm following the case closely."

"All right, I'll play. What do you know about the killer?"

Wolf made a clicking sound with his tongue.

"Only what the newspapers report."

"You're bullshitting me."

"A better question: what have *you* ascertained about the Golden murderer, Scarlett? After all, it's up to you to catch him."

Bell hesitated, unsure how much she wanted to tell Wolf.

"Go on, Agent Bell. I won't bite."

The fog swirled around her knees as she glanced back at the motel. No Gardy, no prying eyes.

"A crown of thorns. What's the significance?"

A moment of silence, then…

"He adorns his victims with a crown of thorns? Intriguing."

"He might place the crown post mortem."

"Jesus's enemies placed the crown upon his head to mock him. Our killer has religious issues, but thorns signify many things."

"Sin and sorrow?"

"Very good. You've done your homework."

"Significant for the victim or the killer?"

"Without more information I cannot say. Tell me, Scarlett. How does he display the bodies?"

Display the bodies. Wolf knew more than he let on.

"He perched her in a cornfield in place of the scarecrow."

Wolf hissed. In the background, Bell heard another noise. Wind?

"Arms outstretched as though hung upon a cross?"

"Yes."

"Left for the crows to pick her eyes clean. Our killer's deep-seated anger bonds with religion."

"Like God's Hand."

"I doubt our man believes himself an avenging angel, Scarlett. No, he's more complex than that. You'll have to dig deeper. Displaying the body tells me he's making a statement. Needs attention."

Bell slumped against a tree and leaned her back against the trunk, her head submerged beneath the mist.

"He sent a photograph of the victim to the FBI."

"As you discovered her?"

"Yes."

"Bold. I wouldn't suppose Harold tracked the email."

"This guy's smart. He loaded the photo onto a website and bounced it through multiple servers. We're waiting for him to make a mistake, but I don't think we'll catch him that way."

"No, you won't. Understand why he displays the bodies as he does and you'll find your killer." A pause. "Scarlett, I could join you on this investigation. Our two minds together...he wouldn't stand a chance."

"I have a partner, Wolf."

"Do you now?"

The motel's outline disappeared and reappeared in the swirling mist. She couldn't see Gardy's room, only the glow of the vending machine outside his door.

"How could you know Gardy and I aren't on the same page? You're following me, dammit."

"Neil Gardy lacks your imagination and talent, Scarlett. He'll never live up to you."

"He's the senior agent."

"In name only. Tell me, Scarlett. When you broke the neck of Alan Hodge, where was Gardy? Wrapped around a tree, I believe."

Bell swallowed. There was an accident. But that information never made it to the press.

"And when you gunned down William Meeks in California, did you not save your partner's life in the process?"

"He took a bullet for me."

"Neil Gardy takes a bullet for no one. Carelessness got him shot. God's Hand. William Schuler. All your heroism. It was I who pulled Gardy to safety after Schuler knocked him unconscious. Should have left him to die. It would be one less anchor around your neck."

Biting off a sob, she dried her eyes.

"Don't say that."

"But it's true. The world would be a much simpler place if we spoke the truth more often."

"Gardy's a good man."

"Is he, Scarlett? Are you certain no skeletons lurk in Neil Gardy's closet? If you venture inside his empty apartment in the dead of night, trawl through his belongings and see the wolf without its sheepskin, you might not like what you find."

"Sure you're not talking about yourself?"

A dry cackle.

"If you wish to find the fair teacher alive, you'll accept my aid."

"How did you…we haven't released…"

"I'm coming, Scarlett. See you soon."

CHAPTER ELEVEN

Night is at the window when an odd discomfort pulls Clarissa Scott awake.

She droops over. Bindings catch her before she falls. Ropes tied around her chest and legs clasped at the ankles, arms splayed to either side with her wrists pinned to a rough, scratchy surface. Wood shaped into an X. No, not an X, but a cross. The texture is rough through the bare skin of her back.

He stripped her. Left her naked except for her bra and underwear.

She yelps and wiggles her feet. Searches the gloom for the kidnapper and sees a video camera on a tripod aimed at her from across the room, a blinking red light above the lens signaling the camera is running. A cable snakes from the camera into a daisy chain of electronic equipment, one box she identifies as a computer. Drives whirl and grind as the machinery renders her in digital bits. And she thinks, where does the video go? Corrupt voyeurs enraptured by torture pollute the Internet. Now she's the star of their sick show.

Then she suddenly remembers where she'd seen the man before. Several months ago a man came to the school to fix her computer. Something about the network not connecting properly. He'd spent an hour inside the classroom, just the two of them, the children downstairs for physical education. When she tried to converse with the man, he averted his eyes and gave timid, one-word answers as he concentrated on the task at hand. Afterward, he left with barely a word, and that was the last she saw of him, though the computer worked liked new and no longer slogged through websites.

Did he target her? How long has he planned this?

Wind rattles the windows. She yanks at the bindings, but they hold her tight. In the dead of night, the *whump whump whump* sound repeats. Something she's heard a hundred times without giving it a second thought. Her mind races too fast to zero in on the source of the noise.

Scott gasps. She hadn't seen the man beside the window until now. He staggers out of the shadows and stands beside the camera.

"Please, whatever you want. I'll give you money. Don't hurt me."

Pleading will get her nowhere. Instinctively she knows this, yet she hopes she can appeal to him on a basal level, sway him to keep her alive long enough until…

Until what? Nobody knows she's here, wherever here is.

"I know you," she says, sniffling. Tears clog her eyes, turn the room blurry. "Golden Central School. You worked on my computer."

He studies her with increased curiosity, though he doesn't reply. Now and again he peers through the camera's viewfinder, makes certain the equipment is working, the focus razor-sharp.

"You were polite, I remember. Nice. You wouldn't hurt someone."

The lens rotates. Zooming in.

"Why are you doing this? I was kind to you."

He turns the lens to the wall. The floor shakes as he storms at her. She flinches, unable to move. When the maniac stops, they stand nose to nose, the man's breath puffing against her face.

"Now the world will watch you pay for what you did to me."

He reaches into the dark and yanks something sharp and spindly off the table. Thrusts it toward her face as she turns her head and clamps her eyes shut.

Cautiously she opens them. Recognizes the thorns, now shaped into a circle and woven upon one another. A crown, she thinks with a shudder.

He places the crown upon her head. Thorns yank her hair from the roots, scrape her scalp, dig into the thin layer of flesh. She moans, not wanting to give him the satisfaction of watching her cry. Warmth trickles down her cheeks and rides the curve of her scalp to her neck.

Unsatisfied with the fit, he jiggles the crown and sets it to his liking. Each twitch tears her head and invokes fresh pain. Pleased, he backs toward the camera, never pulling his eyes away.

He drops to a knee and types a string of characters. The computer responds with a green button prompt upon the screen. Moving the mouse, he clicks the button, and an adjacent monitor fires up with a live picture of Scott suspended and bleeding.

"They can see you now."

The maniac and camera divides Scott's attention, both leering at her out of the gloom. The ropes dig her wrists. Burn.

As she fights, the crown plunges down her tilted head and draws bloody streamers.

CHAPTER TWELVE

In her dream, Bell ran through a black forest of nightmare limbs, the branches claws that tore clothes and raked her eyes. A man pursued her through the dark. Her semi-conscious mind, the lone rational voice which understood this was just a nightmare, worried she'd never rid her dreams of God's Hand. He closed the distance with each step, and in the strange way of dreams, she realized her pursuer was not God's Hand but a new threat. One she hadn't considered.

I see you, Scarlett, the voice whispered against the back of her neck. But when she twisted her head around, the forest path was clear.

She broke into a meadow of switch grass and blue moonlight. The desolation exposed her.

Weaponless, Bell spun in a circle. The pursuing footsteps no longer followed through the forest, yet she sensed eyes watching her.

She took one step before the gunshot exploded down from the heavens and clipped her shoulder. The momentum twisted her around with a spurt of blood. She dropped to one knee, panting, scanning the night for the shooter.

She ducked below the second shot and felt the bullet singe her hair. The shots came in rapid succession, forcing her face down against the muddy earth. The noise grew into thunder.

BOOM BOOM BOOM

She sprang awake with a gasp as the explosions followed her out of her dream. Reaching through the dark for the Glock, she checked the cartridge and aimed it toward the source of the sound. Logan Wolf? Her heart was a trip hammer through her chest and lungs.

"Bell, it's me. Open up."

"Gardy?"

Bell exhaled and lowered the gun. Her hand trembled as she flicked the table lamp on. She rubbed her eyes against the harsh light assailing her.

"Bell, open the door."

"I'm coming," she said, sliding into her sweatpants.

She padded across the room. Before she opened the door, she checked the peephole and saw Gardy standing in the walkway, his laptop cradled under one arm, his eyes scanning the parking lot.

She unlatched the bolt and let him inside.

"Why were you pounding so loud? You'll wake the dead," she said, checking the parking lot. Theirs was the only vehicle in the lot.

"I knocked for five minutes. You didn't hear?"

"No...I mean, I might have," she stuttered, remembering the nightmare gunshots.

"What?"

"Never mind."

"It doesn't matter. You need to see this."

Gardy swept the empty food wrappers off the table and laid the laptop in the center. She circled around to Gardy's side while he typed his password.

A cluttered room of light and shadow appeared on the screen. Bell couldn't take her eyes off the woman, head slumped over as though dead, arms stretched to either side. Camera lights pulled the woman's form out of the dark.

"Harold has been running scans all night," Gardy said, stretching the video window so it filled the monitor. "He followed a suspicious link to this site. Bell, there are over two thousand people watching this."

A counter on the bottom of the screen updated as viewers joined and departed the morbid presentation. With the picture zoomed in, Bell discerned a shallow rise and fall from the woman's chest. Stripped and degraded, but still alive.

"That has to be Clarissa Scott. She's suspended the way we found Shelly LaFleur."

"Like a scarecrow."

"I don't think he sees her as a scarecrow."

A crown of thorns angled from the top of Scott's head to her eyebrow. Dark streamers followed the thorns across the woman's face. They barely glistened in the light, suggesting the blood had dried.

"Why can't Harold find the source?" Bell asked, though she knew why. The killer covered his digital tracks.

"If there's a way, he'll find her. In the meantime—"

"There is no meantime, dammit. She's dying." Bell grasped the laptop and spun it toward her. She dropped to her knees and brought her face closer to the screen. "Is there sound?"

"It's on."

She clicked the controls and amplified the volume to its maximum setting. If the killer was inside the room with Scott, he remained silent.

Scott suddenly hitched. Bell jumped at the noise.

"Can you enhance the sound?"

"Not from here. They're working on it at headquarters. If they get anything, Harold will send us the audio files."

The likelihood the video originated within a ten-mile radius of Golden drove Bell to the edge of insanity. So close, yet he hid in plain sight. Zooming the video to double size, she studied the room, searching for anything that hinted at the killer's location.

"Why is it we can trace a goddamn phone call but we can't track a lunatic with a computer?"

She trembled with helpless fury. Gardy lowered the screen and touched her shoulder.

"We'll find her, Bell. I promise. Right now I need you to be calm. Focus on what we can control."

It was the first time he'd been civil to her since the Logan Wolf argument. She harbored pent up anger, yet the shared crisis and common goal of bringing Clarissa Scott home alive reunited them, if only for a moment.

The problem was Bell couldn't control anything. The killer taunted them, laughed in their faces.

Gardy opened the laptop, pausing until certain Bell wouldn't launch into another tirade. Placing her hands on her hips, Bell walked in a circle from the bed to the table, then back again. Perhaps they could trace the killer by bandwidth usage. Unlikely. Kids playing shooter games taxed the Internet more than one guy with a video stream.

Gardy lifted the phone to his ear when a familiar noise drew Bell's attention. It might have come from the hard drive as Gardy's laptop churned, except it grew and diminished as she played with the volume controls.

"Hold on for a second," she said, and Gardy clicked off the call and lowered his phone. "What's that noise?"

"I don't hear anything."

"It repeats in waves. Listen."

She raised the volume to maximum amplitude and stood back. There it was, plain as day. *Whump whump whump.*

Gardy squinted and stroked his thumb across his chin.

"Weird. Maybe we're hearing the computer or servers."

"I don't think so."

She continued to listen, and she could see Gardy's curiosity growing.

"I swear that sounds familiar," he said, and she nodded. "Keep listening. I'll call the office and have them zero in on the pattern."

Bell knelt before the table and stared at the screen. Clarissa Scott's life hung by a thread. But for how much longer?

CHAPTER THIRTEEN

The briefing room inside the County Sheriff's Department was smaller than the break room. A running joke around the office stated you could fit two chairs and a card table into the room, but if you added the cards, you'd break the fire code.

Barely enough space existed for the deputies. A table outside the room featured coffee and three boxes of donuts. Deputies Rasovich and Monteville each grabbed a pair of glazed donuts, while Greene licked frosting off his fingers and sipped coffee, staying out of the way of the others.

Inside the briefing room, an LCD screen hanging over the podium simulcasted the video coming into Gardy's laptop. The feed died once per hour when the video switched to a different home on the dark web. Harold's skill allowed him to locate the new site within fifteen minutes, but to do so he needed to follow the path of detritus left behind by voyeurs on message boards. When he didn't find it, an anonymous email arrived, mocking him with a direct link.

Clarissa Scott hung limp on the video screen, a

scarecrow close to death throes, gaunt ribs poking out below a spill of black hair. The crown crept over one eye, and Bell worried Scott would jolt awake and expose her eye to one of the wicked thorns. For now, the woman's chest swelled and receded, proof Scott still lived. Sheriff Marcel conferred with Gardy off to the side. They both gave Bell furtive glances as they spoke. She tried to ignore them.

When Marcel called his deputies into the room—they all carried coffee now, Rasovich's face sunken as though he'd gone on a bender last night—they shuffled inside with concerted effort not to look at the video. Greene pulled his gaze away, horrified and embarrassed, and sat with his head down and his hands clasped between his knees.

"You're all aware of the situation," Marcel said, adjusting the podium's microphone upward. "So I won't waste any time. The only goal is to find Clarissa Scott alive, so I'll turn it over to Agent Bell with the FBI's Behavioral Analysis Unit."

The deputies whispered as Bell took her place behind the podium. A step stool lay at her feet, but she chose to lower the microphone with her head poking over the podium.

"Good morning. The BAU lab obtained the link to a private video feed after midnight this morning. We have verified the woman in the picture is Clarissa Scott." Murmurs rippled through the room. Marcel drove his hands down to silence the room. Bell finished her introduction before transitioning to the profile. "The unknown subject is a large man. He'd need to be to prop Shelly LaFleur on the scarecrow post. The killer is intelligent, possibly a genius with computers, but in public he's a ghost. He goes out of his way to avoid conversation, keeps his head down, eyes on the floor. Based on an eyewitness account from yesterday morning, it's possible the killer drives a black 4x4."

Rasovich spoke up.

"You just included half the county."

Monteville laughed.

"Be that as it may, it's a lead, and we need to follow it. Back to our unknown subject. His anger ties with religion. The crown of thorns is significant. In the bible, Jesus's enemies placed the crown upon his head to mock him for claiming to be the son of God. But some believe the crown of thorns symbolizes sin." From the shadowed corner, Gardy glared at Bell. This was the first time he'd heard a theory regarding the crown's symbolism. "Perhaps a religious figure victimized our unknown subject."

"We're checking into molestation cases involving area churches over the last twenty years," Marcel added.

"Good. The FBI is running their own checks. Between both our efforts, we should find something soon if the killer grew up in this area. Keep in mind we're grasping at straws, and parts of the profile don't add up. If a male priest molested our killer, it's likely he'd direct his anger at other males, particularly those in positions of authority. Instead, he's targeting women."

"Could be he's angry at his mother," Marcel said, itching his head uncertainly.

"Go on."

"Well, maybe a religious figure molested him as you suggested. First thing he'd do is go to his mother. What if she called him a liar?"

"Or blamed him. Very good, Sheriff." Marcel sat up a

little straighter. "In addition to the religious angle, the deputies are following potential leads regarding the missing dogs. While we haven't identified a common thread between the families, one exists. It's up to us to find it."

Rasovich said something under his breath and brought a snicker out of Monteville. Something about wasted time and government incompetence. Marcel shook his head at them, and Bell continued.

"As for the video, our tech team is fighting to trace the link, but as was the case with the photograph of Shelly LaFleur, the unknown subject switches the pictures from one website to another while bouncing each website among different servers. He must be using an algorithm. Otherwise, he'd need to stay awake constantly and wouldn't have time for the victim."

Marcel asked, "At any point, has the killer entered the shot?"

"No. He's either careful to stay out of the picture or content to stand back and let the world see what he's done. Already, a few video snippets leaked and went viral. The networks picked up the story as well."

More murmurs, this time laced with anger over the press sensationalizing a local murder and abduction. Marcel attempted to regain order so Bell could continue, but Monteville already had his hand in the air.

"Yes, Deputy Monteville?"

Monteville stood up from his chair.

"I'll acknowledge the elephant in the room. Are we sure this guy didn't already kill Scott? This might be a video playing on a continuous loop."

Rasovich nodded, and Greene glanced at Bell with the

frantic hope the BAU could verify Scott lived.

"We considered that. The lab is compiling the video as it comes in. On time lapse, shadows receded through the room consistent with sunrise, though he blocks the light. We think the killer drapes the windows to keep the room dark. And to conceal his activities."

Bell opened her mouth when the burner phone buzzed in her pocket. It was dangerous to carry the burner with Gardy standing a few steps away, but if there was one thing she could say about Logan Wolf, the man didn't make idle threats. She looked out over the deputies' faces and half-expected to see Wolf staring back at her.

Bell cleared her throat and excused herself from the podium. Gardy raised an eyebrow and mouthed, "you okay?" The blood drained from her face.

The burner buzzed again. Insistent.

"That's all for now."

Confused banter followed Bell as she rushed for the hallway. Someone grasped her arm, and she swiveled around to Gardy staring at her.

"What's gotten into you?"

"Nothing, Gardy. You need to let go of my arm if you don't want me to puke on your shirt."

He released her arm and stepped backward. Marcel rushed into the hall beside Gardy.

The sheriff asked, "She okay?"

Bell locked the door to the women's room before Gardy replied.

The phone rattled like an angry hornet when she pulled it from her pocket.

"This better be important, Wolf. Do you know how many cops I'm surrounded by now?"

She assumed he knew the precise number of deputies inside the briefing room. Had the restroom possessed windows, she'd expect to glance through the glass and find him staring at her. A chuckle came from the phone.

"Time ticks away for Clarissa Scott, Scarlett. Our killer means to flay her in front of the world."

"If you're watching the stream, you're as guilty as the miscreants getting their kicks off torture porn."

"No more guilty than you, dear. How does it make you feel when you see her tied to a stake?"

"You're sick."

"And you're asking the wrong questions. Enter the killer's mind. Identify his motivation and anguish."

Bell checked her face in the mirror. Black crescent moons, the price paid for lack of sleep, formed beneath her eyes. She ran the faucet and splashed water on her face.

"If you know who he is and you're holding out on me —"

"Dear Scarlett, I would never hold out on you. I'll help you catch him, but first you owe me a profile."

The profile of his wife's killer. She'd given the matter a great deal of thought during quiet times over the last month. Unconvinced a serial killer murdered his wife, Renee Wolf, Bell believed someone Logan Wolf knew killed her.

"Tick-Tock, Tick-Tock. Your answer, Scarlett?"

Placing her ear against the door, Bell listened for conversation outside the restroom. The hall was quiet, Gardy and the sheriff having moved on.

"Fine. Where shall we meet?"

"I'm inside your motel room now."

CHAPTER FOURTEEN

During her trip back to Golden, Bell fought to keep control of the wheel. The few vehicles she encountered on the desolate county road appeared to hurtle at her like shooting stars. She couldn't think straight when she imagined Logan Wolf inside her motel room.

After hiding in the restroom, she'd discovered Gardy in the break room with Marcel. Since they were due to break for lunch, nobody objected when Bell suggested she make a run to the drugstore. Medicine to settle her stomach, she lied. Gardy nodded and said he'd phone her with a meeting place after lunch, yet a strange fire burned behind his eyes. She never saw him blink.

Every several seconds she checked the mirrors. No one followed. She almost wished someone had so she wouldn't need to face Wolf alone.

When she pulled into the motel parking lot, another vehicle slumbered outside the last room on the right. But this was a minivan with banal stick figures adorning the rear window: a man, a woman, one girl, two dogs. Not the ride of choice for the nation's most wanted serial killer.

Whatever transportation Wolf utilized, he'd hidden it.

She felt vulnerable, defenseless. Not just because the serial killer waited inside her motel room. He'd found a way inside again. Doors didn't stop Logan Wolf, and the potential always existed for Bell to awaken in the dead of night and find him glaring down at her.

Stopping outside the door, she ran her eyes toward the manager's office and scanned the motel windows. Nobody spied on her. Satisfied, she removed the key from her pocket and turned the lock. She paused and touched the gun. Then she removed the weapon from her holster and moved beside the door, back against the wall.

She shoved the door open and swung the gun into the empty room. Her bed was unmade, the sheet and blanket tangled into a clump at the foot of the bed. The window shade moved. Shadows descended the walls.

Edging the door shut, Bell aimed the gun toward the bathroom. Darkness bled across the threshold. She dropped to one knee and checked beneath the bed. Boards fixed the bed to the floor and prevented anyone from hiding beneath.

"Good afternoon, Scarlett." She hissed and swung the gun. He stood at the entryway to the open bathroom, half in the light, half cloaked by gloom. "No need for weapons. You should know by now I mean you no harm."

"Then why the games? Why not announce yourself the second I opened the door?"

"I needed to be certain you weren't Neil Gardy. Or perhaps the young lady come to clean the mess you made. Have you seen her, Scarlett? I doubt she meets the age requirements, but who the manager hires isn't my business. She's quite young and fetching. She'd look stunning stripped of her clothes and hanging off a pike while crows picked at her eyes."

Bell swallowed the retch bubbling up her throat.

"Stop."

"Would the sight not excite you, dear Scarlett?"

"No."

Wolf glided out of the dark, silent upon the old carpet. A death adder. She motioned with the Glock, a warning for Wolf to keep his distance.

"That's no way to greet your partner. Put the weapon down."

"Gardy's my partner. Not you. Never you."

Wolf tutted.

"A partner is there for you always. A man who vanishes at the first sign of danger but gladly shares the credit for your heroism isn't a man. He's a tick. A parasite feeding off the success of others."

"Liar. He's a good man."

"That good man will run the BAU once Weber moves on. Imagine one of the most powerful men in the FBI, someone who knows your secrets, directing your every move. You'll be his puppet and dance for him."

Bell shook her head.

"What's stopping me from putting a bullet between your eyes? Nobody would question me after they found fugitive murderer Logan Wolf dead inside my motel room."

Wolf grinned.

"You wouldn't kill me, Scarlett. I gave you the name of God's Hand, and I'll bring you the head of Clarissa Scott's kidnapper if you'll allow me."

"Then start talking. How do I find him?"

"You must have leads. Tell me."

Bell leaned against the wall, exhausted from the fruitless search, on guard in case Wolf moved on her.

"Not much. Except a bunch of missing dogs from last year."

"And you think our killer started with animals."

"It's possible."

"No maybes about it. The question is, how did he know the families? This isn't a man who strikes at random. Our killer desired to murder those families and string them up for everyone to see. But he wasn't ready yet. He took the animals instead."

"That's a stretch. We can't find a single link between the families."

"You're looking past the obvious. Put the clues together, Scarlett. You're better than that—"

Wolf opened his mouth and froze. The air felt different, charged with electricity. The doorknob turned. Someone quietly slid a key into the lock.

He grabbed Bell's arm and yanked her back before the door burst open. Gardy shot through the entrance, gun fixed on Wolf's forehead.

"Freeze. FBI!"

Wolf laughed, his black eyes burning with hatred.

"Ah, if it isn't my old friend, Neil Gardy. We were just talking about you."

"Hands in the air, Logan."

Wolf's arms hung at his sides.

"No."

"Don't think I won't shoot. Do as I say. Put your hands in the air."

The room key dangled from Gardy's finger, and as

Bell checked her pockets to verify she still had her key, Gardy pocketed his copy.

"What are you doing with a key to my room?" Bell asked, narrowing her eyes at Gardy.

"Not now, Bell."

Wolf edged closer to Bell, a movement so subtle Gardy hadn't noticed.

"You see," Wolf said, black coat dangling past his hips, hands poised beside the pockets. "This is what I meant about Neil Gardy. He procured a key to your room without your knowledge or consent."

The irony of Wolf's statement bristled her. Many times he'd broken into her apartment or hotel room while stalking her across the country. But that didn't excuse Gardy. She glared at her partner as though seeing him for the first time. Did she truly know him?

"Don't listen to him," Gardy said, reaching for handcuffs. "He might have fooled you, but I've known him too long. Wolf's a murderer. He killed his own wife."

Wolf growled and tugged Bell in front of him. Gardy touched the trigger and halted.

Too late.

Wolf slipped the weapon from his pocket and squeezed the trigger. Bell screamed.

Instead of a gunshot explosion, wires arrowed across the motel room and punctured Gardy above his chest. He dropped to the floor, twitching, drool tricking off his lips.

A Taser.

Bell swung her elbow back at Wolf and found nothing but air. The breeze on the back of her neck told her Wolf had escaped out the door.

She dropped down and yanked the wires off Gardy's

body. He moaned and rolled to his stomach, trying to crawl toward the entryway, body refusing to obey. Bell swung the gun around the jamb.

The parking lot was empty.

CHAPTER FIFTEEN

Ambulance lights flashed across the motel room parking lot as Bell answered questions from Don Weber, the deputy director irate and screaming into the phone.

"Sir, that's not fair," Bell said, cupping a hand over her mouth for privacy. "We have more than enough bodies assigned to the Wolf case. What about Clarissa Scott?"

Arguing with Weber seemed as fruitless as kicking a mountain. He refused to budge before cutting her off mid-sentence and hanging up.

Over a dozen agents were en route to Golden. When they arrived, they'd fan out with local law enforcement and cast a net Logan Wolf couldn't escape from. But they'd never find the serial killer. You only found Wolf if he wanted you to.

Officers from three different police departments and the neighboring county sheriff's office had descended upon Golden by the time the EMT workers declared Gardy healthy. Despite their admonitions to rest a minimum of two days, Gardy strapped the holster around his hip and strode past Sheriff Marcel to where Bell was standing outside her motel room. No sooner did Weber's diatribe end than Gardy's began, and Bell stumbled against the wall from the onslaught.

"Don't give me that shit about being sick. Am I stupid, Bell? I smelled Logan Wolf the second you bolted from the podium."

"Then you followed me."

"You gave me no choice."

"Really? Is that why you made a duplicate of my room key?" Caught off guard, Gardy choked on his reply. "You're worse than an overbearing parent sometimes, Gardy."

"Because of me, you're still alive."

"I was never in danger."

"You're delusional."

"He wouldn't harm me. I realize that's impossible for you to understand, but I'm not his target. Gardy, Wolf was about to help me catch this killer."

"You're a fool for trusting him. Wolf would never aid —"

"He gave me God's Hand's name, or have you already forgotten? And by the way, who pulled you to safety after Warren Schuler knocked you unconscious?" Gardy's expression froze between shock and horror. "Yeah, Logan Wolf saved your life. Think about that tonight when the entire FBI is hunting him down for a murder he didn't commit."

Gardy puffed his cheeks and spun around. Marcel, Greene, and two EMT workers watched the argument. Gardy glared bullets into them until they went about their business. When he spun back to Bell, Gardy took a deep, composing breath, and the beet-red of his face lightened a touch.

"Wolf could have murdered us," Bell said, touching his cheek. Gardy flinched and turned his head. "He chose not to. A Taser. Are you kidding? Not exactly Logan Wolf's murder weapon of choice. If he wanted to slit our throats, he had every opportunity."

"No matter how many times you pet a rabid dog and try to nurse it back to health, eventually it bites."

"Not if I put him down first." Bell met Gardy's glare. "Oh yes, Gardy. The second Logan Wolf moves against me or someone I care about, I'll end this. Permanently."

Gardy strolled down the sidewalk, hands clasped behind his head. The father of the minivan family poked his head out of their motel room. When he saw Gardy approaching, he shut the door and latched the bolt. Gardy's eyes were closed in thought when he returned to Bell.

"Even if I believe this crazy theory about Wolf not killing his wife, I can't protect him. You know what the FBI will do once they track him down."

"Weber made it clear."

"Weber blames me, I take it."

"He blames *us*. I won't cover my ass if it endangers you, Gardy. I'll tell Weber I chose to meet Wolf."

"No. There's no reason to get yourself fired over this." Gardy tapped his foot and glanced around the parking lot. "Here's the story. Wolf followed us to Golden and broke into your motel room. You felt sick, came back to rest, and found him waiting. Every bit of information is truthful."

"Except the sick part."

"What Weber doesn't know won't hurt him. What did he say about the Scott case?"

Bell sighed.

"There is no Scott case as far as the FBI is concerned. It's back in the hands of local jurisdiction."

"So that's it? He redirected every agent to hunt Wolf?"

"Seems like overkill."

"It is, but we don't have a choice in the matter."

Noticing Marcel walking toward them, Bell shifted her body so the sheriff wouldn't eavesdrop.

"We're abandoning an innocent woman, throwing her to the butcher. Marcel's team doesn't have the resources to catch this guy."

"Then our only choice is to catch Wolf and catch him fast. As soon as he's in custody, we can jump back into the Scott case." Bell rolled her eyes and started away. "You intend to play this by the book. Right, Bell?"

"Whatever."

She hopped the curb and angled between two ambulances. Gardy called out to her, but she couldn't hear him over the engines. Damn Weber. If Scott died, her blood was on the deputy director's hands.

No, she wouldn't let Clarissa Scott die.

Their rental SUV sat beside the sheriff's truck. Gardy had taken the keys from her, leaving her without a ride. She surveyed the lot and spied Deputy Greene, sheepish and standing back from the others, hand resting on the gun hilt as if he expected Logan Wolf to explode out of the manager's office with a knife raised above his head.

"Afternoon, Deputy."

Greene touched the rim of his hat and returned to scanning the area. He shot her glances from the corner of his eye.

"I guess the FBI doesn't care so much about a small

town teacher. Just another hick nobody in Washington cares about."

The deputy's words slammed hard into her belly. She figured Greene had read her face during the Weber phone call.

It wasn't fair. Life seldom was. If she had a vehicle…

Greene's truck sat a few parking spaces from Marcel's.

"Would you give me a tour of Golden, Deputy Greene?"

Greene smiled. They climbed into the truck.

CHAPTER SIXTEEN

It was difficult for Bell to hear Gardy over the roar of the engine. Greene swerved around a tree branch, almost causing Bell to fumble the phone.

"Relax, Gardy. I'm taking the route we followed into Golden. Deputy Greene is aiding the search for Logan Wolf."

The curse through the phone suggested Gardy wasn't buying it. She ended the call when the truck clipped a pothole.

"Sorry about that," Greene said, easing off the gas. "This road is a mess. What are we looking for, anyway?"

Bell peered out at the rolling country and wondered what drew her back to this location. A memory from their trip into Golden. A puzzle piece she needed to fit.

"He's out here somewhere."

"The killer?"

"Yes."

"How can you be sure?"

Bell pointed out the window.

"Two abductions in less than a week. That tells me he

needs seclusion."

"Golden is small."

"But the neighbors are nosy. Everyone talks. No, this guy needs privacy to—"

She caught her breath. There. On the hill.

"Take me up there," she said, staring up the incline.

"What? It's just a windmill."

"Hurry, Deputy."

He pressed the gas and turned onto a dirt road, the brown and gray path twisting up the hill to where the sun merged with the horizon. The front of the truck pitched upward at the steepest point and rushed the blood to Bell's head. Then the road leveled out, and they drove beneath the great spinning blades.

"Stop the truck," she said, lowering the window. A storm of dust kicked up as he brought the truck to a halt. "And cut the engine."

Bell climbed out of the car and stared up at the white behemoth. As the wind moved the blades, they clipped the air with a distinctive sound. She immediately recognized it as the background noise in the killer's video. The same noise she'd discerned when they drove into Golden. Why didn't she remember sooner?

Greene climbed down from the cab and met her on the shoulder. Together they craned their necks up at the wind mill.

"Why are we stopping here?"

"There must be a house nearby."

All around them, empty countryside sprawled beneath a sea of blue.

"All I see is goldenrod and hay fever coming on. Should I radio this back to the sheriff?"

Bell chewed her lip. Greene was right. Nobody lived up here.

"Not yet. Let's follow this road and figure out where it takes us."

Greene gave an unconvinced shrug and climbed into the truck. Then they started down the road again, the dust obscuring the way forward and forcing the deputy to run the wipers. Around the next bend, Bell spotted am opening between two trees. A driveway. Had she not glanced down at that moment, she would have missed it.

Deputy Greene backed the truck up and swerved onto the driveway. Bell's flesh prickled. A gray paint-chipped house lay at the end of the drive. No phone or cable lines trailed into the house, but a pair of high-tech satellite dishes extended above the roof. Poplar trees flanked the drive like giant sentries and concealed the back of the house. But Bell spotted the rear bumper of the black 4x4 peeking out from behind the trees.

"Shit, it's him."

Greene swallowed.

"The killer?"

"Call it in."

He fumbled for the radio with shaking hands. Then the bullet blew out the windshield and painted the backseat with Greene's blood.

CHAPTER SEVENTEEN

Everything hurts. As if someone took a club peppered with broken glass and swung it against her forehead. Bell groans and tries to move. Finds her arms bound to either side, splayed, splintered wood digging into her back.

On a subconscious level she senses the danger she's in, but brain synapses misfire and leave her murky and confused.

When someone moans beside her, she remembers what happened to Greene. A gun blast. The accident when the truck hurtled against the side of the house.

Her eyes pop open to a nightmare. The den from the video feed. She twists her head, and knife-like talons from the crown of thorns rake her scalp and forehead, missing her eye by a fraction of an inch.

Keeping her head still, she rolls her eyes to the side. Toward where the moan came from.

And sees Clarissa Scott. Alive, but barely. Bound to the stakes as Bell is. Scott's blood is brown and crusted over like a Halloween disguise. Bell can already feel the warmth of her own blood trickling down her cheeks. A chill rolling over her flesh alerts Bell she's been stripped to her bra and underwear like Scott.

The camera fixes on her. Is the FBI and the world watching her die right now? Below, the computer equipment hums, while the windmill blades taunt her from the hill crest.

"Clarissa. Clarissa Scott, can you hear me?" Black hair clinging to her face like a dead husk, the other woman doesn't respond. "I'm Agent Scarlett Bell with the FBI. We're going to get you out of here."

The words sound ridiculous to her ears, false bravado and delusional. There's no escape. She's as good as dead, just like Scott.

A moment of hope glimmers. Help will come soon. Until she remembers the bullet ripped through the windshield before Greene radioed back to the office.

Greene is dead? The room spins as a wave of nausea clips her.

Maybe the sheriff's department can locate the truck via GPS. Some law enforcement agencies put trackers on their vehicles.

But blind faith will get her killed.

She tests the bindings. Strains. The ropes hold firm and dig into her skin.

A noise comes from above, the strain of floorboards as her abductor paces. Then a shadow descends the staircase.

He's coming.

CHAPTER EIGHTEEN

Gardy shouted into the sheriff's radio, but Bell apparently decided to ignore him. He'd defended his partner to this point. Bell stepped too far over the line this time. He set the radio down when his phone rattled. He glanced down and recognized Harold's number.

"Not now, Harold. I've got a rogue agent to deal with."

"Gardy, you need to open the link I sent you. It's Bell."

Harold's words didn't make sense. Clicking a link would connect him with Bell? As he flipped open his laptop, the cold reality struck him.

"No, no, no," he muttered as the video feed began to load. "This has to be some kind of mistake."

When the image of his broken partner appeared on the screen, Gardy stumbled and fell into a chair. Marcel threw down his radio and hurried to Gardy, the blood draining from the sheriff's face as he looked over the agent's shoulder.

Gardy swallowed. Touching the screen as though he

could shield Bell and protect her from afar, he switched the phone to his other ear.

"How long, Harold?"

"The link came online minutes ago."

"You can confirm its live?"

What he meant was could Harold prove Bell was still alive.

"We think so…it might be a recording but…"

"It's not a recording! She's alive, Harold. I'm looking right at her."

Marcel placed a hand on Gardy's shoulder. The agent flinched.

"Yes," Harold said, fumbling over his words. "She's alive."

"And you'll trace the link."

"I'm doing my best."

"Trace it, goddamnit!"

Silence came from the phone.

"Harold?"

When Harold replied he spoke a hair above a whisper.

"Listen, Gardy. Weber wants everyone on the Wolf case. If he finds out I'm aiding Bell…"

"An agent is in danger. There are protocols."

"Right now Weber doesn't care about protocols. He's seen the feed, and he still wants all resources directed toward apprehending Wolf. I've never seen him like this. Nobody can get through to him."

"That doesn't make sense. Congress will eat him alive when they find out he did nothing to help an agent in danger. He's lost his mind."

"Maybe so, but he's got all of us running scared."

Gardy growled under his breath, and Harold changed his tone. “But I'm staying on this case until we find Agent Bell. I promise.”

“You'd better, Harold.”

Gardy clicked the phone off and yanked his hair.

“You can't help her if you don't think straight,” Marcel said, handing Gardy a cup of coffee.

Gardy pushed the cup away. He couldn't stomach the sight of food or drink.

“Why the hell can’t we find this guy? There can't be more than a thousand people in Golden. If we have to go door to door…”

Gardy trailed off as Marcel snapped orders at his deputies. On the screen, Bell groggily lifted her head as though weights hung off her neck. She stared into the camera. At Gardy.

His fingers trembled as he reached for the mouse. The phone buzzed again, an electric jolt that pulled his attention from the horror movie playing out before him.

He didn't recognize the number and considered ignoring the call. The phone rang again. An angry sound. He answered the phone and barked at the caller for bothering him during a crisis.

“Easy, Neil. You're no good to her like this.”

Stunned, Gardy stood up from the chair and paced to the corner. The others watched him curiously.

“How did you get this number, Wolf?”

“Focus, please. Before you rudely interrupted us at the motel, the wise Agent Bell mentioned missing dogs.”

Wondering if he could trace Wolf’s call before the serial killer cut the line, Gardy recalled the dead end leads. Marcel waved at him from across the room. Gardy shook his head. The sheriff went back to coordinating the search but kept shooting glances at Gardy.

"Yes. The leads hit dead ends. It's not important now. I swear, if you're holding out on me with Bell's location, I'll hunt you down."

"Enough bragadoccio, Neil. It's unbecoming, not to mention you're wasting precious time. The missing dogs, remember. Agent Bell was so close. You both were."

"Explain."

"While it's true none of the families knew our killer on a personal level, they all brought him into their homes. Think, Neil. Name our killer's most impressive skill."

Finding it difficult to hear Wolf over the clamor, Gardy stepped into the hallway. The FBI would take his badge if they discovered the fugitive aided him. To make matters worse, Wolf spoke in circles, bombarded him with a barrage of confusing half-truths.

"Answer the question, Neil."

Gardy shook the cobwebs free.

"I don't know. He's learned to hide in plain sight."

"Simpler than that. Don't be a fool. What's his skill? Even budding serial killers need to pay the bills, Neil."

Helpless to prevent the haunting images from clouding his thoughts, he pictured Bell as he'd last seen her on the video. Bloodied. Close to death. Then it struck him. The killer taunted him with the video feed and pictures, bounced the website around the dark web and eluded the BAU.

"You're saying he's a technology specialist. Someone who repairs computers or sets up networks."

"Very good. But Neil?"

"Now what?"

"If you fail Agent Bell, I'll gut you myself."

Ignoring the threat, Gardy hurried into the operations room.

"Sheriff, the families the deputies interviewed. Give me a name."

Marcel looked at Rasovich. The deputy pulled a stack of papers off his desk and read the first name.

"The Mariano family, Harrington Street."

"Call them," Gardy said, covering the phone with his hand. "Ask them who set up their home network or if someone repaired their computer last year."

As Rasovich dialed, Marcel grabbed the notes and read the next name on the list.

"Adam Ortiz, Elmwood Avenue." Marcel read off the phone number.

Hustling back to his desk, Deputy Monteville recited the number back to Marcel, and when the sheriff gave him a thumbs-up, Monteville picked up the receiver.

As the deputies phoned the other families, Gardy swung outside the door. When he uncovered the phone, the line died.

"Wolf?"

The man Gardy worked beside at the BAU, the country's most dangerous killer, gave him no opportunity to trace the call, and Gardy assumed Wolf was on the other side of the state by now. As he muttered a prayer for Bell, Gardy returned to the operations room and shut the door.

Rasovich snapped his fingers and waved a sheet of paper in the air. Marcel grabbed it from him and read the name.

"Charles Schow," Marcel said.

Gardy repeated the name. "That's our guy?"

"It has to be him."

Gardy typed the name into Marcel's workstation. The address came back a second later.

As Marcel picked up the radio, Gardy ran for the parking lot.

CHAPTER NINETEEN

Each ticking second took a year off Gardy's life. He hit ninety mph on the back roads and nearly lost control on a blind curve. In the mirror, the red and blue lights flashed atop Marcel's truck, the sheriff falling back and surging forward in a desperate attempt to keep up. With Monteville beside him, Rasovich drove another truck a few hundred yards behind Marcel. Several police cruisers rushed toward the hill from across the county, too far off to wait for. Gardy hoped they were smart enough to cut the lights when they neared Schow's home. More than anything he prayed Bell was alive.

At Golden's outskirts, a road branched off and climbed one of the county's loftiest ridges. Gardy stomped the brakes and swerved up a dirt-and-stone incline flanked by overgrown weeds and a throng of buzzing insects. Looming over the SUV, the windmills spun, the blades sweeping down from the sky. He felt very small in their presence. Infinitesimal. He didn't see any houses. Schow's was just around the bend. A good place to hide.

"Got some info back on Schow," Marcel said over the

radio. "He grew up about twenty miles from here in Fairdale. Age of eleven, the kid got caught up in a sex scandal at his church."

Gardy slowed the vehicle, aware he was close to the turn.

"Priest?"

"No, one of the sisters. Never heard of such a thing. The human race creates its own monsters, Agent Gardy."

"Flashers off, Sheriff."

Marcel doused the flashers behind Gardy, then it was just the two vehicles creeping down a road devoid of human life. He caught sight of the driveway at the last second and stopped short of the entrance.

Gardy scrambled out of the SUV, gun in hand as Marcel fell in behind him.

Seeing the determined look on Gardy's face, Marcel agreed, "We aren't waiting for backup."

***

To Bell, the man is unnervingly normal in appearance. Taller than the average man, yet indistinguishable otherwise. A deadly chameleon.

He checks the camera, the computer, the network feed, then types a command. His eyes follow the swarm of characters scrolling down the screen.

Bell hangs on the posts, arms bound and splayed to either side.

"She's dying, can't you see?"

He ignores Bell's pleading. Clarissa Scott murmurs something indistinguishable. It's the first sign of life from the woman.

"Get her a glass of water. There's no reason for her to suffer." When he doesn't react, Bell glares into the lens. "If you are watching this, my name is Scarlett Bell. I'm an FBI agent. Tell the police I'm somewhere outside of Golden, New York, with Clarissa Scott, a local teacher. We're held prisoner by a white male, approximate age thirty-five years. Brown, curly hair. Height six feet, average build—"

He yanks a patch cord out of the computer. He's killed the audio.

"Nice try," he says, grinning, and types another command. "The audio works on a ten-second delay. Nobody heard you."

His face twitches, and Bell knows she rattled him. He might be bluffing. And even if he isn't, a good lipreader can pull the information off the video feed.

Scott moans, anguished. Against her bindings, the woman stirs.

"You're not alone, Clarissa. I'm not leaving without you."

A shadow rolls down Bell's face, and she turns her attention back to the maniac. He's stalking toward her, the camera lens pointed down at the rug. This is it, she thinks. He'll murder them now. Suffocate them the way he did Shelly LaFleur, then string up their carcasses outside Golden and let the vultures feast.

"Stay away, you son-of-a-bitch."

Bell yelps as he clamps his palm over her mouth, the other hand pinching her nostrils shut. The loss of oxygen is sudden and shocking. Her body writhes, eyes bulge as the maniac smothers the life out of her. He cannot kill her instantly. It will take four or five minutes for him to suffocate her. This knowledge cannot stand against the explosion of panic rippling through her body. Her eyes meet his, and she sees no remorse, no sadness, only an insane need to watch her die at his hands.

She bucks her body against the ropes. Squeals as the splintered posts dig into her flesh.

How long has it been? One minute? Already her strength saps. Along the periphery of her vision, Scott twitches as she awakens.

Emboldened, the killer becomes careless. He turns his back on Scott and shuffles too close to her bound hands. With the man's shirt riding up his belly, Scott claws his exposed back. Nails dig deep and draw blood.

The man spins and smashes his fist against Scott's jaw. Her head rocks back. Blood spurts from her mouth and sprays a red, dripping slash against the wall. But Scott is awake now and screaming into the maniac's face as Bell dry heaves from sucking air back into her lungs.

The hands clamp over Bell's mouth and nose again. He's positioned himself to the opposite of Bell so Scott cannot reach him, and when he shoves his palms down, something cracks in Bell's nose. Blood fills her nostrils and flows down her throat.

Defenseless, Bell quivers. Her vision darkens, sounds grow muted. Even Scott's screams seem to come from a great distance.

Then all she sees is the red hatred of the maniac's eyes. Bell no longer struggles. She'll die at his hands.

An explosion she cannot place jars her. Her face drips with blood.

But the blood is not hers.

CHAPTER TWENTY

Bell gasped when the killer's grip weakened and slipped off her mouth and nose. His hand touched his side and came away red. As he stared into his palm in disbelief, legs trembling to hold his weight, another explosion rocked his head sideways and crumpled him.

The camera crashed to the carpet as Marcel rushed to stand over Schow. At the entryway, Gardy lowered his gun, arms hanging at his side like they were stapled at the shoulders.

The sight of Bell shocked Gardy into blinking twice. Sirens approached from the distance, and two additional figures—Monteville and Rasovich—waded into the house of horrors.

"For Pete's sake, is someone going to untie them?" Marcel said, the gun poised over the still breathing killer.

Unfrozen, Gardy ran to Bell as Rasovich aided Clarissa Scott. Monteville joined the sheriff. The tension on Monteville's face promised he'd squeeze the trigger if the killer moved.

"Nice shot, Gardy. I always said you were the second

best shooter in the FBI."

As though he missed the joke, Gardy concentrated on untying the bindings while trying to ignore her exposed body.

"I thought I'd lost you and..."

Gardy's throat closed up while he unraveled the ropes. She shivered, and he removed his jacket and placed it over her blood-smeared chest.

"You'll ruin it. That's an expensive jacket."

A smile curled his lips. He glanced surreptitiously over his shoulder, then leaned in to whisper in her ear.

"Bargain rack at Target."

He pronounced Target as *tar-jay*.

The last binding unraveled, Bell slipped off the wooden posts. Gardy caught her before she tumbled over, and as she found her sea legs, he helped Bell to her feet.

"Goddamn cop killer," Monteville scowled.

The deputy begged for an excuse to pull the trigger and avenge Greene, whose body lay outside, slumped over the wheel in the crumpled truck. He didn't need an excuse. Schow's breathing ceased. The maniac lay still beside the purring computer equipment with the camera aimed down at his head.

"Deputy Greene?" Bell asked, praying the gunshot was only a nightmare, her mind playing tricks on her.

Gardy shook his head. Bell slid down the wall and came to rest on the floor, knees drawn up.

Two police officers, strong-looking males not long on the force, arrived next. Three paramedics joined them seconds later. As the officers led a bloodied Clarissa Scott outside, Marcel knelt beside Gardy and Bell. The sheriff's eyes misted over, and Bell knew he was thinking about his sister.

"Here you go," Marcel said, dropping Bell's clothes in her lap. "The boys found them in the next room along with the teacher's."

The perfect gentleman, Marcel pulled his eyes away, though Gardy's jacket only left Bell's legs exposed.

"Thank you, Sheriff. I'm sorry about Deputy Greene. He died a hero."

Marcel removed his hat. He ran his hand through hair which seemed to gray by the minute.

"That he did, Agent Bell. That he did."

The sheriff excused himself and walked outside.

"Maybe you should get dressed," Gardy said, offering his hand.

Cupping her clothes to her chest, she took his hand and followed him into the vacant bedroom toward the end of the hall. He turned his back when she handed him his jacket. When he started for the door, she grabbed his arm.

"Hey, Gardy."

"Yeah?"

"I'm sorry for the way I've been acting."

He lowered his head.

"Don't be sorry. Seems I should be the one apologizing."

A moment of quiet fell over the room. Murmurs from the den drifted through the home like memories.

"Yeah, you really should. You've been one hell of an ass-hat lately."

He stumbled at the door and grimaced. A grin broke across his face.

"Takes one to know one," he said, stepping outside and edging the door shut.

It was then she realized she was alone in Schow's house. Goosebumps covered her body.

"Gardy, can you leave the door open a crack?"

"Sure thing."

"And stay outside the door?"

"Of course. Ass-hat on guard."

She chuckled, and for a brief second the levity helped her forget where she was and how close she came to dying.

But as she pulled her clothes on, she pictured Greene. So young. Certainly his parents brimmed with pride over their deputized son. Their boy died today. Someone would have to tell them.

Bell thought it should be her.

CHAPTER TWENTY-ONE

The sun hovered low in the sky when the last of the crime techs filed out of Charles Schow's little home. Gardy waved to Marcel as the sheriff drove off. They'd meet him at the office in an hour.

Yellow police tape covered the door. The tape flapped whenever the wind blew, and that made Bell think of the windmill and why she hadn't identified the sound sooner. She realized such thinking was the path to madness, and no guarantee existed a deputy wouldn't have lost his life storming the house if she'd figured it out sooner.

"Don't go there," Gardy said, reading her mind. "Schow would have seen us coming. He rigged cameras around the property and monitored everything from his den. Only reason he didn't spot me running up the porch was—"

"Yeah, he was busy killing me." Bell shrugged. "I led Deputy Greene into an ambush."

Gardy set his jaw and looked away. She could tell he was frustrated. Yet he let her vent and purge her guilty mind, and she appreciated him for it.

When Bell gathered herself, Gardy had his hands on his hips, staring off toward the rolling hills, everything tinted red beneath the sun's last stand.

"You know why we found you, right?"

Bell walked over to Gardy.

"No."

He opened his mouth, stopped, and licked his lips.

"Wolf called me."

"How did he get your—"

"Don't ask. It's probably best I never find out. He connected the dots when I couldn't. The missing dogs, in particular."

"I remember. The deputies didn't find anything when they followed up with the families."

"We didn't ask the right questions. The video feeds and server bounces should have clued us in. Schow was a genius with computer technology."

Nodding with understanding, Bell said, "He worked for the families. Around here, Schow was the only choice if you ran into trouble with your PC."

"Turns out he fixed Clarissa Scott's school computer. Scott remembered him."

"Jesus."

Gardy gave her a knowing look. "Marcel sent Monteville back to LaFleur's house. Inside the bedroom, he found a laptop with a sticker affixed to the shell."

"Let me guess. Schow configured her computer, too."

"That's how he chose his victims."

The light began to fail. Shadows crept across the lawn, claiming Schow's murder house as their own.

Gardy kicked at a rock. "You know I can't protect Wolf."

"I know."

"Between local law enforcement and the FBI, they sealed the perimeter air-tight."

"And yet they won't catch him," Bell said, peering out over the silhouetted hills. "We tried for over a year."

Gardy looked doubtfully at Bell, seemed to reconsider, and nodded his agreement.

"You really don't believe he murdered his wife."

"I don't. Nor did I imagine the special ops shooter who tried to kill us outside Bealton. I never told you this, but the sniper shot Wolf that night."

Gardy followed Bell's gaze to the horizon. His jaw shifted in thought. Soon they'd need to explain to Weber why they chose to rescue Clarissa Scott after he ordered all agents to contain Logan Wolf.

"What are we going to do, Gardy?"

"I don't know. But whatever happens next, know I'll be by your side."

***

Ready for the next Scarlett Bell thriller?
Read **Dark Waters - Book 9**
Available on Amazon

Let the Party Begin!

I'm a pretty nice guy once you look past the grisly images in my head. Most of all, I love connecting with kickass readers like you.

Join the party and be part of my exclusive VIP Readers Group at:

WWW.DANPADAVONA.COM

Show Your Support for Indie Thriller Authors

Did you enjoy this book? If so, please let other thriller fans know by leaving a short review. Positive reviews help spread the word about independent authors and their novels. Thank you.

Author's Acknowledgment

The Scarlett Bell series would not be possible without the encouragement, support, and efforts from my patrons.

Tim Feely
Lisa Forlow
Steve Gracin
Michelle Kennedy
Dawn Spengler

I value each one of you more than I can express.
Thank you for believing in me.

Why Novellas?

The world of entertainment has changed. While I enjoy movies, I watch Netflix series and comparable programming more frequently. Movies are too short to match the story and character arcs of a well-written series, and that's why I favor a long series of novellas over a few novels.

I prefer a long series which I can lose myself in, but broken up into smaller, manageable episodes that don't take up my entire evening.

In short, I'm writing the types of stories I enjoy and composing them into forms I find preferable.

I sincerely hope you enjoy the Scarlett Bell series as much as I love writing it.

How many episodes can you expect? Provided the series is well-received by readers, I don't foresee a definite end and would prefer to expand on the characters and plot lines for the foreseeable future. I still have plenty of devious ideas for upcoming stories.

Stay tuned!

About the Author

Dan Padavona is the author of the The Scarlett Bell thriller series, Severity, The Dark Vanishings series, Camp Slasher, Quilt, Crawlspace, The Face of Midnight, Storberry, Shadow Witch, and the horror anthology, The Island. He lives in upstate New York with his beautiful wife, Terri, and their children, Joe, and Julia. Dan is a meteorologist with NOAA's National Weather Service. Besides writing, he enjoys visiting amusement parks, beach vacations, Renaissance fairs, gardening, playing with the family dogs, and eating ice cream.

Visit Dan at: www.danpadavona.com

Made in United States
North Haven, CT
16 April 2024

51349127R10082